OUTSIDE
NOWHERE

BY ADAM BORBA

The Midnight Brigade

Outside Nowhere

OUTSIDE NOWHERE

ADAM BORBA

ILLUSTRATIONS BY SAM KALDA

LITTLE, BROWN AND COMPANY

New York Boston

Little, Brown and Company
Hachette Book Group
1290 Avenue of the Americas, New York, NY 10104
Visit us at LBYR.com

First Edition: October 2022

Little, Brown and Company is a division of Hachette Book Group, Inc. The Little, Brown name and logo are trademarks of Hachette Book Group, Inc.

Library of Congress Cataloging-in-Publication Data
Names: Borba, Adam, author.
Title: Outside nowhere / Adam Borba.
Description: First edition. | New York : Little, Brown and Company, 2022. | Audience: Ages 8–12. | Summary: After setting off one too many pranks, Parker is sent to work on an unusual farm in the middle of nowhere where something extraordinary is growing underground.
Identifiers: LCCN 2021054989 | ISBN 9780316542647 (hardcover) | ISBN 9780316542654 (ebook)
Subjects: CYAC: Farm life—Fiction. | Self-actualization (Psychology)—Fiction. | Friendship—Fiction. | LCGFT: Novels.
Classification: LCC PZ7.1.B6695 Ou 2022 | DDC [Fic]—dc23
LC record available at https://lccn.loc.gov/2021054989

ISBNs: 978-0-316-54264-7 (hardcover),
978-0-316-54265-4 (ebook)

Printed in the United States of America

LSC-C

Printing 1, 2022

FOR HENRY.
AND FOR CHARLES AND HAZEL
WHO SAVED US.

1

THE POOL SMELLED like chlorine and fruit punch. It had always smelled like chlorine, but it only began smelling like punch the morning Parker Kelbrook showed up to work as a junior lifeguard.

Parker was a good-looking kid. Trim and athletic, though he didn't play sports. Perfect hair, though he never seemed to brush it. And surprisingly stylish for a boy his age. When he was eleven years old, he borrowed his grandfather's tweed sport coat after becoming chilly at the Pennsylvania State Fair. Though the jacket was a tad large, it suited Parker so well that his grandfather insisted he keep it. From that day forward,

Parker dressed exclusively in formal and casual wear from decades past purchased at local thrift shops.

The boy was arguably overdressed in a corduroy blazer at the Pittsburgh Leisure Centre's pool, but he was the only member of the summer staff who wasn't cold.

Sometime around 6:45 AM, Parker managed to pour the Leisure Centre's entire supply of Purple Madness Fruit Punch Mix off the high board. Fifty-seven gallons of powdered punch sank toward the drain, then bounced off the bottom of the pool into an indigo cloud. As the cloud expanded it turned the water a subtle shade of purple. The fruit punch mix was supposed to last the concession stand the whole summer. The purple stain it left on the pool's tiles was potentially permanent.

—

The Leisure Centre's young assistant manager sat behind the desk in a cramped office. His head in his hands, his breathing heavy. The floor littered with cleaning supplies and pool toys.

"Obviously I have to fire you," the assistant manager said to his shoes.

"Is it obvious?" Parker asked, loafing in front of

him. "This is a really comfortable chair. Did you buy this?"

The assistant manager lifted his head. "It was here when I started."

"Well, I'm glad they hired you. I haven't been around long, but I can tell you're doing an outstanding job. I bet you become manager in no time."

"I'm just trying to make some extra cash for books and gas before I go back to college." He dropped his head to the desk. "They're probably going to fire me, too."

"Because the pool you're supposed to look after became a giant punch bowl?"

"Yes."

Parker sighed. "I could see that."

"Thanks for understanding."

"So, do I pick up my paycheck from you now, or is that something you'll mail me?"

The assistant manager raised his head and glared at Parker. Parker stared back. Waited. But the assistant manager just held his gaze.

"Maybe I'll go," said Parker. "Seems you have a lot going on."

"Sounds like a good idea."

Parker stuck out a hand and the assistant manager's mouth dropped open.

"I really appreciate the opportunity. Thanks for taking a chance on me. Don't blame yourself. You didn't know better. And I came highly recommended."

The assistant manager nodded, then seemed to surprise himself by shaking Parker's hand.

"Look on the bright side," continued Parker, "now we both have an entire summer to do whatever we want."

Three hours later, Parker and his best friend, Kevin, were eating ice cream in a minimart parking lot with two girls, and a redheaded boy drinking a can of iced tea. Kevin was a lanky kid with dark sunglasses and a waffle cone in each hand.

"My great-uncle Fred has a corduroy jacket just like this," said the girl with the braids. She rubbed a piece of Parker's sleeve between her fingers.

"Sounds like he has incredible taste," said Parker. "Maybe we could all go bowling sometime."

"He's retired in Florida."

"Then he has plenty of time to bowl."

"Are you getting another job?" asked the girl with wavy hair.

Parker smiled and shook his head. "I tried working. It didn't take. Too structured and constricting."

"So you're just gonna do nothing this summer?" said the redheaded boy.

"I wouldn't say nothing," said Parker. "Kevin and I are getting out of town to have a life-affirming amount of fun before school starts."

"Who's Kevin?" asked the girl with the braids.

"Me," Kevin said. "We had three classes together this year?"

She examined his face. "Are you sure?"

Kevin sighed and took a bite from each cone.

"What's everyone doing the rest of the day?" asked Parker. "I know a guy who'll let us borrow a pony from a petting zoo."

"What would we do with a pony?" asked the red-headed boy.

"I was thinking we could sneak her into a movie," said Parker.

"You're nuts," the girl with the braids said with a laugh. "I have to bag groceries."

"I'm tutoring math," said the one with the wavy hair.

"I have to mow my neighbor's lawn," said the red-headed boy. "Hey, do you think they're hiring at the pool now that you're gone?"

"I guess. Want me to put in a good word for you?"

The boy cringed. "That's okay. It's probably better if you don't."

"What do you mean?" Parker asked.

"Uh. Nothing," said the redheaded boy. "It's just that you're not exactly the greatest reference."

The others became fascinated by their ice creams.

"Why would you say that?" said Parker.

"Seriously?" said the redheaded boy. "You ruined their pool. They probably won't hire me if they know we're friends. No offense. I should get going. See you around."

Parker wrinkled his nose. "Um. Okay."

The girl with the wavy hair finished her cone. "Yeah, I'm late. We should go, too."

"Bye, Parker," said the girl with the braids.

"Bye," he said with a grin.

"I'm here, too, you know," said Kevin.

"Bye, Devin," she responded as they walked away.

"It's Kevin," he mumbled before taking a massive bite of ice cream. "I don't understand why they always like you."

Parker gave Kevin a playful punch on the arm. "I'm sure they were intimidated by your mysterious sunglasses."

Kevin forced a smile.

6

Parker sensed that his friend was feeling unsure. "You just have to be a little more confident. They weren't lucky enough to grow up next door to you, so they have no idea what a prodigy you are at board games and Ping-Pong. Girls love that stuff. It's how my grandparents got together."

Kevin laughed. "It's called table tennis."

"Sure it is. What time are we leaving on Saturday?"

"Early. My mom wants us in the car by nine. Did you ask your dad?"

"He'll be fine. I mean, he'll miss me, but how could he say no to me spending a month at the beach? He knows the Outer Banks is the only place where I can really unwind. I can't wait to do nothing on a lounge chair."

Kevin's mouth twisted. "I was kind of planning on getting a job at the surf shop down the street from the house we're renting. Our landlord knows the lady who owns it and says she could let me work a few hours a day."

"Really?" Parker frowned. "Maybe you can ask to work mornings and I'll sleep in?"

"Oh. Maybe."

"This is going to be the best summer of our lives," Parker said as he ate a spoonful of mint chocolate chip.

"Are you sure your dad is going to be okay with you coming?"

"Don't worry about it." Parker looked across the parking lot to the shops lining the boulevard. "I wish I had enough cash to buy new swim trunks."

Kevin bit into one of his waffle cones before tilting his head. "You don't see that every day."

Parker followed his friend's eyeline to a mother walking hand in hand with her five-year-old son. Parker smiled before noticing the little boy's hair was purple. It looked like the kid had been crying.

Parker winced. "Excuse me. Did you just come from the Leisure Centre?"

"I told him the pool was closed," the mother groaned. "But he got excited and jumped in. He used to have the lightest blond hair."

The purple-haired boy looked sheepishly at Parker.

"Let me buy him an ice cream cone," Parker said as he dug for his wallet.

The kid's face lit up.

Kevin took another bite. "Better talk to your dad."

"Just don't let your mom leave without me."

2

AFTER SAYING GOODBYE to Kevin, Parker made his way uptown. Like every Saturday for the previous two years and nineteen weeks, he would have brunch with Ms. Eleanor Birdseye.

The Birdseye mansion sat on eleven of the finest manicured acres in North Pittsburgh. The gates surrounding the estate had been forged a hundred years prior in one of Ms. Birdseye's father's steel factories, and its Corinthian columns were rumored to have been smuggled out of an archaeological dig in Greece. The compound had a staff of eight, which expanded to fourteen during the holiday season. Ms. Birdseye had recently turned seventy-seven years old, but

Parker insisted she didn't look a day over seventy-six. It was one of the many reasons why she enjoyed his company.

The dining room table was covered with stacks of waffles and pancakes, plates of poached eggs, bacon, sausage, three kinds of toast, and five types of jam.

Ms. Birdseye was a tiny woman, hidden behind thick tortoiseshell glasses and the morning newspaper. She scrutinized Parker, who was finishing his ninth piece of bacon. "I don't understand. You quit on your first day?"

"Don't be ridiculous, Ms. Birdseye. I was fired."

Parker spread jam on toast. "This strawberry blend is delicious. Has this always been an option?"

"I couldn't tell you." Ms. Birdseye folded her newspaper and placed it on the table. "I thought that job would be a nice fit."

Parker bit into his toast and shrugged. "Well, you can't be right about everything. Besides, if I were working today, we couldn't have brunch."

"There are more important things in this world than brunch, young man."

"Sure, good company," Parker said with a wink.

Ms. Birdseye shook her head. "Parker, you know I find our conversations delightful. I have since you were a little boy. But I worry more and more about you every day."

"Worry about what?"

"Worry that you have such tremendous potential, but that you're so curiously rudderless. I thought that job would help you."

"Help me? Ms. Birdseye, come on, it's too beautiful a day to be working."

"Sometimes I wish you could be more like my nephew. He's had a job every summer since he learned to ride a bike. But then again, any extended period of time I spend with him bores me to tears. He has the personality of a rusty shovel."

"Sounds like it's best that I stay clear. Did I tell you I'm going to the Outer Banks?"

"The beach?"

"To relax a little."

Ms. Birdseye rolled her eyes. "You've never struck me as someone who needed a vacation. You're still young, but trust me, habits form early. You can't just waste your days away."

"Waste my days away? It's not even noon and I've already taken a nap and had ice cream."

"You had ice cream before brunch?"

"I was worried you wouldn't serve any until dessert."

Ms. Birdseye pursed her lips to hide a smile. "You're an odd duck, Parker."

"Quack."

"You have her sense of humor."

Parker blushed.

"I think that's what I miss most," she continued.

Parker stared out a window.

"Sorry," she said. "I shouldn't talk of sad things on sunny days."

Parker turned back to Ms. Birdseye. Rubbed a sleeve across his eyes. "It's okay."

"You're a good boy, Parker."

He reached for a waffle.

"But I do need to talk with your father about your little science experiment at the pool."

Parker put his elbows on the table and massaged his temples. "I'm sorry about that, by the way. It was dumb. But do you have to tell him?"

"I do. Although first I need to call and apologize to your former employer."

———

Mr. Kelbrook leaned against his kitchen counter opening bills. His fingernails were stained with grease and the word "Birdseye" was stitched above the breast pocket of his navy jumpsuit in yellow thread. "You're not going."

Parker frowned from a stool across the counter. "You're tired. You had a long day. We should talk about this after you've had something to eat. I was thinking we could order pizza."

"We're not doing takeout. And you're not spending your summer lying on the shore in North Carolina."

"Is this because of what happened at the Leisure Centre?" asked Parker.

Mr. Kelbrook exhaled. "Do you have any idea how embarrassing it was to have Ms. Birdseye tell me that my son did *three thousand dollars*' worth of damage to a swimming pool on his first day? She's on the board at the Centre."

"I could see that being a problem," admitted Parker. Then he frowned. "Three thousand seems high, no?"

"They have to drain the water, do a deep cleaning, and then refill it. Three thousand is probably a bargain."

"Is that after subtracting what they owe me?"

Mr. Kelbrook sighed. "You were fired before your shift started. They don't owe you anything."

"Right." Parker grabbed a pen from the counter. Began doodling on the back of one of the bill envelopes.

"Do you realize how lucky we are? Ms. Birdseye doesn't even need a full-time mechanic. She rarely drives anywhere, and I can only wash and wax the cars that sit in her garage so often. I don't know where we'd be without that job."

Parker thought for a moment before nodding. "I know. You're right."

"I mean, she pays your school tuition."

"I told her I was sorry. Anyway, she's the richest person in Pittsburgh and my friend. Money isn't a big deal to her."

"Fifth richest and my boss. And people become rich by holding on to their money. She likes you, but you have to be more appreciative. I wouldn't even have this job if it weren't for your mother—"

"*I know, Dad.*" Parker shrank into his seat. Regretted snapping at his father.

Mr. Kelbrook softened. "I get that things have been rough. They're hard for me, too. But you have to stop doing stuff like this."

"Stuff like what?"

Mr. Kelbrook shook his head at the ceiling. "Things like filling your gymnasium with balloons. Or wrapping your science classroom in cellophane. Or decorating our neighbor's roof with a giant model of the solar system. Or inviting your entire school to a semiformal dance at your vice principal's house. Or having some guy dressed like a chicken sing me a telegram at work."

"Okay, I hear you. But that singing telegram was a surprise for your birthday."

"It wasn't my birthday."

"That's what made it a surprise."

Mr. Kelbrook crossed his arms and stared at his son. "What possessed you to dump a cup of punch mix into the pool?"

"Actually it was almost sixty gallons."

Mr. Kelbrook's head tilted, impressed. "How did you get it all onto the high board?"

"I can accomplish anything I put my mind to."

"It's a shame you put your mind to doing as little as possible."

"Like most things, that's a matter of perspective. I'm tired. I need a break this summer."

"A break from what? You've never worked a day in your life."

"That's a matter of perspective, too."

Mr. Kelbrook set the bill on the counter and grimaced. "I wish that were true. Parker, you have more going for you than any kid I've ever met. You can grow up to be anything you want."

"Thank you."

"I'm just worried you're on a path to choose nothing. You used to be so motivated. When are you going to start taking things seriously again?"

"Taking things seriously makes them real."

"Life is real, Parker."

"Life is unfair."

"Sometimes. But we have to roll with it anyway. Why did you take the job if you didn't want it?"

"It was before I knew Kevin had a spare room at his beach house. I guess I figured I'd be spending the summer at the Leisure Centre regardless, so I might as well get paid for it. But then they gave me the early shift. Why would I want to go to the pool before my friends got there? Apparently the later shifts are given out by 'seniority.' But there was never any version of me working there long enough for that. They should have just made an exception for me, right?"

Mr. Kelbrook seemed mystified. "That's not really how the world works."

"It's how I like my world to work."

"Well, about that. It's not going to anymore."

Parker stopped doodling. "Are you making me get another job to pay for the pool?"

"Of course I am."

Parker got up, walked around the counter, and put a hand on his father's back.

"Look, I love you, but if you let me go to the Outer Banks with Kevin there's apparently some surf shop that I can maybe work at for a couple of hours a day. I can pay it off in no time. Or at least by the end of next summer. Don't make me spend the whole summer here."

"I love you, too. But you're not spending the summer with me."

Parker beamed. "You're letting me go to the beach with Kevin?"

"Not even close."

17

Parker slammed a suitcase shut at the foot of his bed. "This feels like a terrible mistake."

"It'll be good for you," his father called from the kitchen.

Parker zipped the duffel bags at his feet. "How do you know? You hadn't even heard of this place two days ago."

"Because Ms. Birdseye said so," said Mr. Kelbrook.

"Does it matter that I don't want to go?"

"Not particularly."

"Okay, but to be clear, I'm going to say it for the twenty-seventh time—I *really* don't want to go."

Silence from the kitchen.

Parker frowned. "I'm not sure Ms. Birdseye's decision-making skills are what they used to be. She means well, but she's getting up there in age."

"Has she ever steered you wrong?"

Parker thought for a moment. "There's a first for everything."

"Hurry up and finish packing."

Parker's shoulders deflated. He glanced around his room. Spotless as usual. An antique desk, a hat rack draped with baseball caps and fedoras. Framed photos surrounded a mirrored dresser. He lifted one of the photographs—a laughing woman eating cotton candy.

He had her eyes.

Mr. Kelbrook stepped into the room. Froze when he saw Parker holding the photo. "Oh. You know, you can go say goodbye to Mom before I drop you off at the station. If you want."

"Um, maybe."

"I could drive you?"

Parker stared at the picture. "That's all right. Thanks."

Mr. Kelbrook nodded. "Okay. Dinner's ready." He headed down the hall.

Parker slid the frame into a pocket on the suitcase before following his father. He bumped into his dresser on the way out the door. Resting below the mirror was a brochure with a picture of a stunning farmhouse and three tiny figures crouched in a field.

3

PARKER THOUGHT RIDING on a train for two nights would be fun. He was wrong.

It had been a day and a half since Parker left Pittsburgh, and at least twenty hours since he had seen anything outside the window resembling a city. He hadn't even spotted a building since breakfast. What he *had* seen was corn. Endless stalks of corn. Corn racing by at seventy miles per hour. And corn inching along whenever the train slowed to a crawl for reasons that would never be known to him.

When Parker squinted and slouched, the tops of the cornfields almost looked like the sand dunes that led to the shoreline at the Outer Banks. Almost. He was figuratively and literally heading in the opposite direction from that North Carolina beach where he was supposed to spend his summer.

When his father had said he'd bought him a fifth-class train ticket, Parker figured he was joking. Something like that couldn't possibly be real. He was wrong about that, too. His seat didn't recline. The food cart only sold stale cheese sandwiches. And he hadn't managed to sleep for more than six minutes at a time.

Oh, how he missed sleep. Every time he drifted off, he was shaken awake by a sudden jolt of the train, or a kick to the back of his uncomfortable chair by one of the twins behind him. He had given up on asking their mother for help after her third "They're two years old, what do you want from me?"

As Parker shifted uncomfortably in his seat, he regretted not seeing his own mother before leaving. Visiting tended to put him in a bad mood afterward, but it usually helped to spend some time with her and talk. She always understood him better than his father. And though she wouldn't have changed his father's mind about how he'd spend his summer, it would have been nice to vent.

Parker wanted to get up to stretch his legs, but he worried he would wake the elderly man who had fallen asleep on his shoulder. He wished the man would stop drooling. Parker slipped a cocktail napkin between himself and the man's mouth.

Three days earlier, Parker had found a seersucker suit with thin blue and white stripes at a thrift shop. He was proud of the discovery, especially since it was on the clearance rack and his size. It wasn't long before he had serious regrets about wearing a full suit on the train. He was roasting.

The sun pounded on Parker through the window. The humidity was ruthless. The air as sticky as the floor. And since there wasn't anywhere for that air to go, it was hot during the night, too. Sometimes it even felt like there was heat coming off the moon. He would take his suit jacket off if it weren't for that elderly man's face pressed against it, and the cringe-able amount of sweat that would be visible through the white shirt he wore underneath. So he left the jacket on and continued to bake. It was a vicious cycle.

For some reason Parker had been under the impression that entertainment would be provided on the trip. Perhaps movies. Maybe a magazine published by the train filled with interesting articles about traveling by rail. There was nothing of the sort. Instead, Parker stared straight ahead and counted the tiny polka dots on the upholstery of the seats in front of him. There were 6,709 dots visible on the chair directly ahead, and 6,511 dots on the one next to it. He confirmed those numbers nine times.

Things went from bad to worse when the twins and their mother got off the train, only to be replaced by the trash from the third-class car's lunch service. The smell of leftover tuna fish and mayonnaise made him equal parts nauseous and starved for anything other than a stale cheese sandwich.

The train rolled over a bump that shook the elderly man awake. Parker watched as he found his bearings and wiped the sleep from his eyes. The man looked down between them and frowned. "Would you mind taking your elbow off my armrest?"

Parker glanced at the sliver of seersucker resting on the divider between their seats. "No problem," he said as he pulled his arm away and folded his hands in his lap.

The man rolled his eyes, yawned, returned his head to Parker's shoulder, and went back to sleep.

Parker's summer vacation had taken a disappointing turn.

～

Forty-eight hours after leaving home, Parker's train arrived at his destination as the sun rose. He wouldn't have known if the conductor hadn't told him. It didn't look like a station at all. Just a bench next to an empty ticket office. The office wasn't much bigger than a telephone booth. The ground beneath the bench wasn't even paved. It was like whoever built the station threw the office and bench off the back of a truck and called it a day.

The conductor came by again and nudged Parker's arm. "Come on, kid, get moving. Train has to go."

Parker sighed. "It's been a pleasure," he whispered to the sleeping man before extracting himself as gently as he could.

It felt wonderful to stand. And even better to step off that humid train into a summer breeze. To breathe something other than that fifth-class train air.

Parker was the only passenger to disembark. Within seconds, the train's whistle blew twice and it began chugging away. He smiled before turning to the dirt beneath his feet.

Parker's eyes went wide and he spun in a circle, searching frantically. His hands shot into the air.

"Wait!" he yelled as he sprinted after the train, his necktie waving over his shoulder.

But the train didn't wait. No matter how many times Parker called for it to stop, or how quickly he ran,

the train became smaller and smaller until he couldn't see it anymore.

Eventually he stopped running. Rested his hands on his knees and caught his breath.

Then he looked around again.

There wasn't a soul in sight. And no sign of a highway. Only a few dirt roads and a set of train tracks that ran through cornfields on the horizon.

With no one to pick him up, and no clue where to go, Parker sluggishly returned to the bench and lay down in his seersucker suit.

The suit was now his only pair of clothes.

Parker's luggage was still on the train.

He fell asleep in seconds.

4

"NICE SUIT."

He heard her words before his eyes opened. When they did, it took him a moment to decide he wasn't dreaming.

Staring down at him was the face of a girl about his age with the perfect amount of freckles. It was a distinction he was unaware someone could have until he saw her. She wore overalls and a flannel shirt. The shirt's sleeves were rolled up to reveal small, muscular forearms.

"Thanks," he replied.

"I was joking. You look ridiculous."

"Oh." He sat up. "I'm Parker."

"I figured."

He stuck out his hand and they shook. His shoulders twitched as something caught him off guard. He admired her sun-kissed hand in his. "You have strong hands for a girl."

"You have soft hands for a person."

Parker shook his head. Popped up from the bench. "Sorry. I'm tired. That was supposed to be a compliment. It came out wrong."

"Mine came out as intended." She examined the ground. "Travel light?"

Parker sighed. "I left my stuff on the train."

"Interesting choice."

"I thought a porter or something would bring it down for me," he said with a shrug.

"It seems that wasn't the case."

Parker grinned. "Yeah. Seems not."

"Why would you think that?"

"I guess I didn't give it much thought. My dad always handles the luggage."

"I have a hunch it's going to take you a while to fit in here."

"I don't mean to come across as arrogant, but people tend to like me."

"That did sound arrogant."

"Just give me time. I'm charming. Trust me." He smiled. She didn't. Parker took another look around. "So what exactly am I doing here?"

"You don't know?"

"I only know I'm supposed to spend the summer working on a farm halfway across the country from my house."

She nodded. "You're an expert. When we get there, I'll call your dad to let him know you got in safely. Let's go. We've got a long walk." She headed toward one of the dirt roads through the cornfields. "I'm Molly, by the way."

"Nice to meet you, Molly."

She didn't respond. He hurried after her.

⌒

Beads of sweat trickled down Parker's brow as he followed Molly up that dirt road. He wasn't sure how long they had been walking. Maybe an hour? Maybe twenty minutes. The road was flat, but his feet were killing him. He had never been able to find comfortable dress shoes from a thrift store. He'd almost worn tennis shoes on the train but had decided it would cheapen the look of the suit. Now he wished he had chosen differently. He felt blisters forming on his heels as he loosened his tie.

28

"You should take your jacket off," Molly called back.

Parker glanced at the soggy shirt under his suit. Grimaced. "I can't."

"Why not?" she asked without turning around.

"I'm afraid I'm a bit underwater."

She exhaled and kept going. "You're going to sweat a lot while you're here. You should start getting used to it."

Parker took a deep breath. Took the jacket off and folded it over an arm. He felt exponentially better but couldn't wait to take a shower.

Molly glanced back. "You really are a sweaty mess. You should have kept that jacket on."

Parker smiled. "You from here?"

"Topeka."

Parker looked around, like doing so would provide a clue as to where that was in relation to them. All he saw was corn on either side of the road, and miles of dirt in front and behind them. "I never really paid attention during geography. So...close?"

"That's relative. About fifty miles."

"What's it like?"

"It's like a hundred thousand salt-of-the-earth people surrounded by cornfields and cows."

"Amazing."

"If you say so."

"I'm from Pittsburgh."

She kept walking. Parker brushed some sweat from his forehead. Jogged a bit so he could walk alongside her.

"Nice hustle, Parker."

"Is it much farther?"

"That's relative, too."

Parker puckered his lips. Thought about how to rephrase his question. "Do you know how many more minutes we'll be walking?"

"Getting tired?"

"No. I was—"

"It's just up here." Molly turned to her right.

"Where are you—" Parker stopped as she walked down an unmarked road between the fields, which seemingly came out of nowhere.

At the end of that road was the stunning three-story green farmhouse from the brochure, with a matching water tower and a barn. A maple tree with a tire swing grew to its left. Beyond the house were acres and acres of farmland. A corral held horses, goats, and cows. It was all surrounded by a blue picket fence. It was picturesque. The kind of calming thing someone would paint and hang in a doctor's waiting room. Certainly not anything Parker had ever seen in person. It wasn't a beach house, but things were looking up.

"Welcome home," Molly called over her shoulder.

5

AS THEY APPROACHED the farm, Parker noticed a handful of boys in the field. While the cornstalks he had seen on the journey stretched over his head, whatever was growing at this place seemed to be recently planted. The crops only stood a few inches tall.

"What are you farming here?" Parker asked Molly.

"Hope and second chances."

"Those are high in fiber, right?"

He strained to get a better look at the boys in the field. They didn't seem much older than him. A couple seemed younger.

The farmhouse's front door opened and Parker's jaw dropped as a monster of a man stepped out. Like everyone else there, he was clad in flannel and denim. The man had to tilt his head to fit under the house's doorframe. Parker focused on the man's frown.

"Where's his luggage?" barked the Farmer.

"He left it on the train," called Molly.

"Why did he do that?"

"I'm still not entirely sure, but he thought someone would carry it down for him."

The man grunted. Did an about-face, tilted his head, and went back into the house, the screen door slamming behind him.

"He seems like a lot of fun," said Parker. "Is he still mad at that kid for planting those magic beans?"

Molly didn't smile.

"I'm assuming the cows and goats are here so he can gobble them up for breakfast," Parker continued. "I thought Cyclops only had one eye. What time do the villagers come by to do the human sacrifices for his family?"

"He's my uncle," said Molly. "Let's find you some clothes."

Parker's face fell. "Oh. I didn't—"

"You talk a lot, Parker."

⌐

33

Sunrays crept through the gaps between the slats of the shed behind the barn, lighting up the dust particles that danced through the air.

The shed was stacked floor to ceiling with supplies. Shovels, garden hoes, rakes, buckets, work gloves... and dozens of trunks and containers.

Molly dug through an ancient trunk. Pulled out a couple of pairs of jeans, some overalls, a red flannel, a blue flannel, and a green-and-white one. Shoved them all into Parker's arms.

"These will be a little big, but they should be fine if you roll them up."

"Appreciate it," said Parker. He smelled the moldy old clothes. Forced a smile to hide his repulsion. Molly didn't seem to care.

She looked at his scuffed-up dress shoes and shook her head. Turned to a rack of boots. Grabbed the smallest pair and tossed them onto Parker's stack of clothes. "Mingo can buy you some socks and underwear when he goes to town tomorrow."

"Thanks. Who's Mango?"

"Mingo. He helps run the farm for my uncle. Think of him like a camp counselor. You'll meet."

"Sorry about earlier. I was just joking around."

"I know. I wish you were funnier."

"Me too, but I make up for it with this incredible smile."

He grinned.

"You have something in your teeth." She pushed past him to the shed's door. "Come on. Let me introduce you to some folks."

Molly headed out, the door closing behind her. Parker leaned in to check his reflection in a clasp of one of the newer trunks. Opened wide. Saw that his teeth were clean. Shook his head.

As he hurried after Molly, one of the boots fell from his arms. He awkwardly bent over and put it back on his stack. Used a foot to push open the shed door.

Outside he saw Molly talking to a couple of boys caked in dirt. The larger boy stared him down over Molly's shoulder. He was built like a football player. His blond hair cut close, and his biceps visible through his flannel. The other boy was tiny. Short in stature, not much meat on his bones, and small facial features. His head was shaved. He smiled and waved, which prompted Molly to turn.

"Parker, this is Chet and Walter. Chet and Walter, Parker. Parker's from Pittsburgh."

The larger boy scowled at Parker. "What's up with the suit, Big City? You look like a ventriloquist dummy."

"Was about to change," said Parker.

The larger boy sneered. "Did you fall in a lake?"

"Just got a little hot," said Parker. "You must be Chet. You look like a Chet."

"I'm Walter," said the larger boy. "You look like a Chet."

"That's fair," said Parker.

"I'm Chet," Chet said with a grin.

"Hi, Chet," said Parker.

"Hi," Chet chirped.

Walter rolled his eyes and stomped off toward the field.

"Chet can get you settled and teach you the rules," said Molly. "I'll go help the two-eyed Cyclops call the train about your luggage."

"Sorry again. I'm sure he's great. And I'll be more responsible going forward. I promise I'm going to be one of your favorite people in no time." Parker smiled.

Molly shook her head as she walked off to the farmhouse.

"We should get moving," said Chet, heading to the

barn. "We're way behind today because the cows got out again."

"Huh?" said Parker.

"Yeah, last night," said Chet. "So annoying." Chet pushed his way into the barn.

Parker followed Chet inside. What presumably once held animals had been remodeled to house people. The room resembled army barracks. Six cots were lined in two rows of three, a trunk at the foot of each bed. Two sinks stood at one end of the room (Parker noticed there wasn't a mirror above them). One long table was against a wall, and a round table with folding chairs sat across from it. At the other end of the barn, a door to what must be a bathroom. The view through the front window was the dirt road he had walked in on and walls of corn growing on neighboring farms. Out the back window was the field. Parker's heart sank as he took in his home for the summer.

"We don't sleep in the farmhouse?"

"The farmhouse? Nah. That's more of an office and a place for Boss and Molly. One of the rules, actually." Chet crouched in front of a cot by the bathroom door. Opened the trunk. It was empty inside. "This one can be yours."

"Thanks," said Parker as he placed the hand-me-downs in the trunk. "So, what are the rules?"

"Pretty easy, man. One: stay out of the farmhouse. Two: do your chores. And three—and this is the big one—don't eat the crops."

"Don't eat the crops?"

"Don't eat the crops," confirmed Chet.

"That's it?"

Chet scratched his head. "Yeah, I guess. And then there are unspoken rules like try to be nice to people and clean up after yourself, but I think Boss thought those were a little too obvious to be official rules. So that's it, man."

Parker nodded. Tried to get a handle on Chet. He seemed like an earnest straight shooter. And he enjoyed the younger boy's use of the word "man." "Did you say the cows got out? Is that, like, code for something?"

"Code? No, man. The gate on the corral isn't the greatest, and it busts open if Martha sleeps against it."

Parker frowned. "Martha?"

"Yeah, Martha. The big cow. Luckily the goats didn't go, too, this time. Sometimes goats can be lazy to your advantage, you know?"

"Without question," said Parker.

"Normally Mingo deals with the animals by himself—and he's good. But there's only so good a person can be when cows get their own ideas, right?"

"Of course."

"So, anyway, we had to spend the whole morning trying to push the cows back into the corral. And the cows here are just as stubborn as anywhere else, so we're way behind today."

Parker stared at Chet.

Chet stared at Parker.

Chet shrugged. "You should get changed."

Parker nodded. Grabbed a pair of jeans and the red flannel and stepped to the bathroom door. "Let me rinse off," he said.

He pulled open the door to discover a single toilet in a tiny room. A broom and a dustpan leaned against a corner. Parker was confused. "Where's the shower?"

Chet looked at Parker like he was speaking another language. "Shower? It's behind the corral. But the pump gets turned off after breakfast."

"Wait. Is the shower *outside*?"

"Yeah. But don't worry, man, the water is colder than a lonely chipmunk on Valentine's Day—you won't want to be in there very long. Mostly we use the hose on the side of the barn. Or the sinks." Chet pointed across the room.

Parker exhaled. Glanced at his arms, sticky with sweat, and tugged the shirt clinging to his body. He headed toward a faucet. "Give me three minutes."

6

"MUCH BETTER," SAID Chet as Parker stepped from the barn. Chet held a bucket in each hand.

Parker's jeans and flannel were about eleven sizes too big. They must have belonged to the Farmer. After splashing sink water on himself, Parker spent most of his time getting ready rolling up his sleeves and the cuffs of his pants. He could easily fit an extra person in his shirt. He was used to wearing clothes that were slightly oversize, but these were absurd.

"Here," said Chet, holding out one of the buckets. "We pull weeds on Mondays."

Parker frowned at the bucket. "Pull weeds?"

"Yeah. On Mondays."

"What's fun about that?"

"Fun?" Chet strained his arm to inch the bucket closer to Parker. "I don't know, man. Is pulling weeds supposed to be fun? Do you want to…"

Chet wiggled the outstretched bucket.

Parker reluctantly took it. "So we're supposed to do real work here? I thought this was going to be more like summer camp."

"They don't make you pull weeds at camp?"

"Well, I've never actually been, but I'd be surprised if they made you pull weeds."

Chet nodded to himself. "Yeah, man, I've never been, either, but I'd be surprised to hear kids had to pull weeds there, too. Did you want to grab gloves from the shed?"

Parker gazed at the shed. "To pull weeds?"

"Yeah, man. I don't use gloves, but your hands look kind of soft."

Parker flinched. Glanced at his hands before throwing his shoulders back. "I'm good. Let's just get this over with."

Chet seemed skeptical. "You sure?"

"Totally. Let's go."

"If you say so, man." Chet led the way toward the field. Exchanged waves with a couple of boys heading to the supply shed carrying shovels over their shoulders. One tall and skinny, with tightly coiled hair hanging over his ears. The other with straight black hair and baby-face cheeks. They seemed to be about a year older than Parker. He gave them a nod.

"That's Tyrone and Carlos," explained Chet. "They're always together. They're nice. You'll meet them eventually."

Parker and Chet came to a stop in the shadow of the water tower at a fenced-off section of the farm about the size of a football field. Two dozen rows of plants stood a few inches high. Each row about as thick as one of Parker's strides.

"So what kinds of things do we grow here?" asked Parker.

"We only grow radishes," said Chet.

"I've never understood radishes."

"They're a root vegetable," explained Chet.

"I meant the taste."

"Oh. Well, that won't be a problem, man," said Chet as he hopped the fence. "Remember, we can't eat these."

Parker climbed after. Took a closer look at the rows

of radishes. Each plant no bigger than his fist, a scrum of leaves sprinkled with dirt. Beneath the leaves, the tops of pink roots peeked from the ground.

Parker took a sniff and cringed. "Are these even edible? Or are they for, like, cleaning supplies or something? They smell a little funny."

"Someone said they add their scent to natural gas so people know when there's a leak because natural gas doesn't have a smell. I think they do it in a factory or something? Like a science factory? I don't know, man. I guess there are places that exist just to put smells into stuff. Feels like a big business. People like to smell things, you know?"

"Preaching to the choir. I love to smell things," deadpanned Parker.

"Me too," said Chet. "Just don't eat them. Let's get pulling."

Parker ran a hand through his hair, then scratched the back of his head as he looked down at the large weeds growing alongside and between the row of radishes at his feet. There was one every couple of steps. "Is there a trick to this?"

Chet squatted in front of the next row over. Pulled a weed. Tossed it in his bucket. "Trick? Kind of hard to pull a weed wrong."

"Got it," said Parker as he bent over and pulled a weed from the top. It ripped free at the base, and he dropped it into his bucket.

Chet watched as Parker moved forward a couple of paces and did the same thing to a few more weeds.

"Wait, man. I take it back," said Chet. "You're doing it wrong."

Parker stared at the weeds in his bucket. "What do you mean?"

"You have to pull them from the *base*, not the top, or else you leave the roots and they grow right back." Chet demonstrated for Parker, pulling from the base, bringing the weed and a trail of roots with it.

Chet pointed behind Parker. "You have to dig those roots out now."

"Oh."

"And see those little sprouts?" asked Chet. Parker looked closer to see a dozen little plants growing between the weeds he had pulled. "Those aren't tiny radishes. Those are weeds, too."

Parker sulked. "This is a bigger job than I thought."

"That's why I wanted to get moving."

Parker nodded, took a couple of steps back, crouched. Began pulling the smaller weeds. Did some digging to get the roots he missed on his first attempts.

Tossed them in the bucket. Saw Chet working quickly and pushing ahead on his row.

Then he looked up at the vast field of radishes in front of him. He sighed. Even with Chet moving twice as fast as him, it would take hours to finish.

His hands already hurt.

—

Parker was startled by the clang. He looked up from the field to see the Farmer ringing a bell on the side of the house.

"Lunch," said Chet from a few rows over.

Parker watched as the other boys made their ways toward a picnic table by the barn. He stood to follow. Upright, he realized how sore he was.

"Hey, man," called Chet. "We kind of have to finish this whole thing. What do you think about pushing through lunch so we can relax before dinner?"

Parker eyed the field. He'd never been more exhausted in his life. Thanks in large part to Chet, they were halfway done. Knowing himself, Parker had to admit that it might be hard to get going again if he took a break. Maybe Chet was right and they should keep working. But another feeling overtook that one: "I haven't eaten much the last couple of days."

"Dinner is the big meal. Let's keep moving. It's just cheese sandwiches for lunch on Mondays."

Parker laughed to himself. "Then I'm definitely good. Cheese sandwiches was all you had to say."

He glanced at his bucket. Weeds were nearly overflowing. "What do we do when our buckets get full?" He surprised himself with how much pride he felt from asking that question.

"Already?" Chet shrugged. "Did you try stomping down on it?"

Parker looked at the full bucket. Dropped a boot in the middle. What was almost spilling over became less than a quarter full. "Oh." He stared into the bucket. "Never mind."

Parker squatted and started pulling weeds again.

His hands felt raw.

An hour after the others finished lunch, Parker pulled the last weed from the last row. He chucked the weed into his bucket, wiped the sweat trickling down his face, and brushed his dirty hands onto his jeans. He popped up and smiled. Chet was already climbing the fence.

"I honestly didn't think I was going to make it," said Parker. "I can't wait to lie down." Parker was so excited that he practically sprang over the fence. His legs ached when his feet landed on the other side.

"Lie down?" asked Chet as he squatted at the first row of radishes on the other side of the fence. "I said we had to do the whole field."

"What do you mean? We just—" Parker stopped as he processed the other three sections of the field. All three the same size as the pen they'd just finished.

Parker's breathing got heavy and his world spun. He fought the urge to scream. He shook his head. "Nope. No, no, no." He grabbed his bucket and stomped toward the farmhouse. "No, no, no, no, no."

"Where are you going, man?"

"Home. I don't belong here."

"But we have to finish the field."

"We don't. I'm done."

The Farmer stood in front of the house with his arms crossed, staring down at Parker, who had changed back into his seersucker suit and a T-shirt.

"I just need a ride to the train station."

"Train won't be rolling back for a few more days," grunted the Farmer.

"Well, then I need a ride to Topeka or Wichita or someplace where I can hop on tonight." Parker paused for a moment as something occurred to him. "Obviously I'll need to borrow some cash for a ticket, too. But I can mail you a check when I get home. As soon as I have some money."

"No one has ever tried to quit so early."

"It's not that I'm quitting," Parker explained. "I'm not supposed to be here in the first place. There's been a misunderstanding. This isn't what I signed up for."

"Your father signed a contract on your behalf. You will honor that contract."

"See, that's the thing. He clearly didn't comprehend what he was signing. My father would never do something like this to me."

"You're right. There is a misunderstanding. He's not doing it to you, he's doing it for you."

"That's clever. I appreciate that. But trust me, my dad would never send me to a place like this if he knew what it was."

"It's a farm. And one that your father's employer has been supporting financially for years."

Parker's face fell. "Ms. Birdseye owns this place?"

"We assisted her late husband years ago. She's been

48

our most supportive benefactor ever since. I agreed to take you on as a favor to her."

"Well, that changes things a little." Parker sighed. "Wait. You helped her late husband with radishes? Like with a really big salad? I don't see how—It doesn't matter. Look, honestly, I'm too tired to do any more work today, and I'm sure Ms. Birdseye wouldn't want me to overexert myself. Why don't we pick up this conversation tomorrow? I'm spent."

"Get back in the field."

"I feel like you're not listening to me."

"Get back in the field."

Parker stared at his hand-me-down boots. "I just can't do it."

"I disagree."

Parker shrugged. "I guess we're at an impasse."

⌒

Carlos and Tyrone leaned against the blue fence with their mouths open. Walter watched from the barn's doorway and shook his head before going inside.

The Farmer strode across the field carrying a bucket in one hand and Parker in the other. The boy was tucked under his arm like a newspaper.

"Put me down!" yelled Parker.

"Stop kicking, you're being absurd," said the Farmer.

"Just take me to the train station," said Parker, seething.

"You seem like an intelligent kid. You have to know that's not going to happen."

"I'm going home."

"You absolutely aren't."

Chet looked up from a row of radishes. "Hey, Parker. Hey, Boss."

"Hey, Chet," said Parker, hanging at the Farmer's side.

"You're done for the afternoon, Chet. Good job."

"Are you sure, Boss?"

"Go wash up."

"Thanks, Boss." Chet stood and grabbed his bucket. Headed toward the barn. "See ya, Parker."

"See ya, Chet," said Parker with a huff.

The Farmer set the bucket down, then looked at the boy under his arm. "We're going to stay out here until this job is finished. If you run, you will waste energy and I will catch you. I don't care if we're here until midnight. But if you focus you can be done by dinner."

Parker stared off at a cornfield on a neighboring

farm. He wondered if he could make it into the field before the Farmer. Wondered if he could keep running longer than the Farmer. He examined the Farmer's muscular physique and long legs. Parker's jaw clenched.

"Do you understand me?" asked the Farmer.

Parker took a deep breath. Glared up at the Farmer. Weighed his options. Determined he had none, which crushed him inside.

"Okay," said Parker.

"Okay what?" said the Farmer.

"Okay, put me down and I'll get back to work."

"Good," said the Farmer.

The Farmer set Parker down. Parker smoothed out the creases in his suit. Took off his jacket and carefully hung it over a blue fence post. Gazed at the enormous field, then turned to the Farmer, who stared back and waited.

Parker sighed, kneeled, and began pulling weeds and tossing them into the bucket.

He moved slowly but pulled the weeds with authority, like he resented each and every one.

The Farmer crossed his arms as Parker steamed in the sun.

The boy continued pulling weeds. He took another look at the massive field and grunted. Then he tried to guess how long it would take to finish. Five hours if he was lucky? Probably more like six or seven. It was hot. He was tired. And he would give anything to get out of the sun and into the shade. He thought maybe if he moved faster he could avoid passing out from the heat.

He pictured Chet's technique, then tried to mimic it to pick up his pace. He used both hands and yanked weeds one after another.

He ignored his aches and pains and focused on the job, and before he knew it, he had completed a row. He grabbed his bucket and moved over to the next.

Then the oddest thing happened. The Farmer kneeled and began to help.

7

PARKER AND THE Farmer walked in silence toward the barn.

The sun had been replaced with a crescent moon. Parker's jacket was back on, and his T-shirt and pants were the color of the dirt in the field.

The boy used both hands to carry the bucket, which was full after being stomped on seven times. His entire body hurt. Even his eyelids and ears. Worst of all, the blisters from his dress shoes now had blisters over them from crouching in his work boots. His feet stung with each step.

The Farmer reached down and grabbed the bucket. "Let me take that. Strong finish today."

Parker was too exhausted to process words. "Huh?"

"You finished strong. That's the most important thing." He gestured to the barn. "Go get yourself something to eat."

Parker only nodded.

The Farmer headed toward the house. Parker went to the barn. Leaned against the door to catch his breath. And for a moment, he was stuck. It felt like his body would crumple against the building. But his intense desire to eat gave him the energy to step back and pull open the door.

"Looking good, Big City!" Walter sneered from the round table. His flannel was unbuttoned, and he rocked on the back legs of his chair. Chet, Tyrone, Carlos, and a longhaired man in his midtwenties sat with him. Empty dinner plates all around.

Parker did his best to smile, but he didn't have the energy to get all the way there.

Chet gave a friendly wave, and the longhaired man stood and approached.

"Hey, bud, I'm Mingo. It's great to have you."

Mingo stuck out a hand. Parker shook it and gasped.

"Ahh, that stings…" He looked down and found his hands covered in blisters, scratches, and cuts.

"Eek," said Mingo. "Those look rough."

Chet cringed from the table. "Probably should have pushed you harder to wear those gloves, man."

Parker blew air through his teeth. "Yep."

"Don't worry, bud," said Mingo. "They'll be back to normal in about a week and they'll just keep getting tougher. I can barely feel my hands anymore."

"Comforting," said Parker.

Mingo nodded. "Let's get you something to eat. You must be starving." He led the way to the long table, which had been set up as a buffet. "Let's see..."

Parker grabbed a plate and scanned the buffet table. The food had been picked dry. The bread basket had a few crumbs. The salad bowl a sliver of lettuce. And whatever had been on the platter was now just a smear of brown sauce.

"Well, hmmm," said Mingo. "Sorry, bud. Looks like we didn't manage the portioning that well. We're so used to it just being the five of us."

Walter rubbed his muscular stomach. "It was delicious, Big City. Almost as good as lunch."

"I thought you had cheese sandwiches for lunch."

"We did," said Tyrone. "But they were brie and bacon. Calling them delicious wouldn't do them justice. They were downright scrumptious."

"Brie and bacon?" asked a disappointed Parker.

"With cucumbers and celery," said Carlos. "That extra little crunch? Just, you know, adds something. Plus, sandwiches are all about the bread, right? Those sandwiches have the best bread I've ever tasted."

"So true," said Tyrone. "There's this little French-inspired baguette shop about ten miles from here that makes their bread and cheese fresh. Mingo rides his bike there on Monday mornings and picks them up for us. It's really quite thoughtful."

"It's just something I like to do for you guys," said Mingo. "Start the week off right."

Parker eyed Chet at the table. "Why would you want to skip that?"

The skinny boy shrugged. "I had an extra piece of toast at breakfast."

"Look how tiny he is, Big City. Does he strike you as someone who cares much about food?"

Chet's cheeks went red. "He has a point, man. Didn't realize how hungry you were or we would have taken a break."

Parker's shoulders slumped before he slid onto one of the folding chairs. "So, there's nothing to eat?"

"Sorry, man," said Chet.

Parker closed his eyes and tried to transport himself to another place. A place with food.

"Oh! What am I thinking?" said Mingo. "Molly set aside one of the sandwiches from lunch for you."

Parker looked over hopefully as Mingo grabbed something wrapped in a napkin from the far end of the buffet table and handed it to him. "It's been sitting out all day, but it's probably better than nothing."

"Thanks," said Parker as he unwrapped the napkin and hungrily bit into the cheese sandwich.

"Might be a little stale," apologized Mingo.

It was. And it was one of the greatest meals Parker had ever had.

———

Parker hosed himself off after dinner, then collapsed onto his cot. He usually had trouble sleeping in a new bed, but that evening he fell asleep shortly after his head hit the pillow.

The pillow was understuffed, only a couple of inches thick. The blanket was itchy. The sheets were scratchy. None of that mattered. Parker was painfully tired.

He woke up once that night. Glanced around the dark room, his head on that thin pillow. The only light came from the moon through the front window.

The others were snoring. But there was another sound.

A baby crying?

He propped himself up on his elbows.

That couldn't be right.

He tried to focus. Listen harder. Which was challenging since he was so exhausted and disoriented.

Then he heard it again. Clearer this time. And closer. "Baa! Baa!"

Parker's head snapped back, startled.

Something appeared in the window. A face?

Was that...

A goat?

He could barely make out its beard and stubby horns in the moonlight.

How tall was that goat?

And it seemed to be moving...up?

Was it...floating?

The goat hung in the window. Its four hooves dangling in the air.

It looked directly at Parker. Held his gaze.

"Baa."

Parker blinked. Wiped his eyes. And went back to sleep.

8

IT TOOK PARKER a moment to remember where he was and shake off his strange dream when he awoke.

He turned to the far end of the room as Chet was stepping out the door. "Wanted to let you sleep, man. But you should get moving. Breakfast. We eat it in the morning."

Parker nodded. Took in the room. The others had gone. Their beds made. He groaned, slunk from his cot, and threw on a pair of hand-me-down jeans, the blue flannel, and boots. Splashed water on his face, patted down his hair, and headed out into the world.

He smiled as he stepped outside. Aside from being

fifteen hundred miles from the ocean, it was a perfect summer morning.

Molly and the farmhands sat at the picnic table eating scrambled eggs and toast.

"It lives," announced Molly.

"Morning," said Parker.

"You look like the incredible shrinking boy in those clothes," said Walter.

Parker looked down at his oversize outfit. Shrugged. "Walter sounds like the name of one of my grandfather's friends. Have you been getting senior discounts your entire life?"

Chet stifled a laugh. Tyrone and Carlos kept their heads down, seemingly not wanting to get involved. Molly sighed and took a bite of toast.

"Are you really making fun of *my* name, Big City? Parker sounds like a valet attendant. That's a job, not a person."

Parker puffed out his chest. "Are we going to have a problem?"

"I can give you one," said Walter as he rose from the table.

Parker was instantly reminded that the boy had at least five inches and thirty pounds on him. Walter was built like an oak tree, an angry one. Parker's face fell and he instinctively took a step back.

"Settle down, guys," said Mingo as he came up behind Parker, put a calming hand on his shoulder, and gave him a plate of eggs and toast.

"Sorry, Mingo," said Walter.

"We okay here?" asked Mingo.

Walter and Parker eyed each other. "We're okay," they replied.

"Okay," said Mingo. "Parker, I'm going to go grab some essentials for you in town. Follow Chet's lead again?"

"Sure, Mingo. Thanks."

"No problem, bud," he said with a pat on the back. "And protect those hands today."

Parker glanced at his mangled fingers and palms. He had forgotten about them for a moment. Nodded as Mingo headed off.

Parker made his way to the others with his plate. Took a seat at the opposite end of the table from Walter.

"Table's getting crowded. Let's get started." Walter stood up and stared down Parker, who took a moment to admire his eggs.

Chet kept eating as Carlos and Tyrone grabbed their

plates and sheepishly followed Walter. "Bye, Molly," said Carlos.

Molly raised a hand in acknowledgment as she finished chewing her toast. Turned to Parker. "I heard from the train."

"Can they pull my stuff and ship it?"

"Not exactly," said Molly. "You're going to have to wait until it rolls back through town."

"How long is that going to take?"

"A little more than a week. It has to go to Oregon and then turn around. I've got the time written in the office. I can take the buggy to the station with Mingo and grab your bags for you."

"Great," said Parker.

"That's assuming none of the other passengers steal your stuff in the meantime."

Parker sighed. "Well, thanks in advance anyway."

"I should get going, too," she said getting up. "My uncle has been manning the phone all night. Better relieve him."

"All night? For, like, emergency radish orders?"

"It's serious business."

"I'm sure," Parker said as he dug into his breakfast and Molly headed to the house.

"Sleep okay?" asked Chet.

"Weird dream," said Parker.

"Happens here."

"Yeah?"

"Yeah. Carlos has them, too."

"What's on tap for today?" Parker asked between bites.

"On Tuesdays we pull weeds."

Parker set his fork down. "Wait. What? We just did that. I thought you said we pull weeds on Monday."

Chet shrugged. "We pull weeds most days, man."

"Are you joking?"

"Why would I joke about pulling weeds?" Chet took another bite of eggs.

"I just don't see—I mean, we spent all day pulling them yesterday. What's the point?"

"We always miss some. And there's good soil here. Things grow faster than usual. But it won't take as long today."

"But we have to do it all over again?"

"Yeah, man. To help the crop grow."

Parker sighed. "This feels like a lot of work just for radishes."

"It's what we do here, man."

"Well, can't we do something besides pulling weeds?"

"Mingo and the other guys are digging up the septic

tank under the old outhouse this morning. You could probably switch with one of them."

Parker grimaced. "Definitely don't want to do that." He felt his body ache. "I just don't think I'm ready to go back out there. Maybe we could take a day or two to recover?"

Chet stared at Parker.

Parker nodded at the barn. "Maybe just take a quick nap first?"

"Boss says we have to work if we want to stay."

"That's the thing," said Parker, "I don't want to stay."

"I have to do it alone if you don't help."

Parker looked at the younger boy and then frowned at the gigantic field.

"Why wouldn't you want to stay?" continued Chet. "There are worse ways to spend a summer."

Parker tried to imagine a worse summer. He couldn't. "Like what?"

"Like sitting on a couch all day, man."

"What's wrong with sitting on a couch? That's what summers are for."

"Well, there are a lot of us on the couch back home. My grandmother maybe only has two or three decades left, so the family spends as much time with her as possible. At any given point, there's usually sixteen, seventeen of us in her living room? Not just summers. My grandmother homeschools us, too."

"Where are you from, Chet?"

"From?" Chet appeared baffled by the question.

"Yeah. Where do you live when you're not here?"

"With my grandmother."

"Yes. Got that. And...where is that?"

"Couple of towns over. My grandmother ran into Boss at the feed store last year and they got to talking. I love my family and all, but this place sure beats sitting on that couch listening to AM radio."

"AM?"

"Yep. Four generations crammed around that one couch, for twelve hours a day, listening to one station with three hours of repeating programming."

"Why don't you change the station?"

"It's my grandmother's favorite. My uncles are pretty protective of that dial. Man, I still can't believe Boss convinced my grandmother to let me come. I honestly don't think my cousin Lenny has ever left the house." Chet breathed in the fresh air and smiled. "I mean, where would you rather be?"

Parker turned and gazed down the dirt road leading away from the farm. Thought of life's endless possibilities.

Then he saw Molly through a window as she climbed

the steps to the farmhouse's third story. He glanced at the scratches and cuts on his hands. "I'm using gloves today."

"Seems like a good idea, man."

⌒

After they jumped the blue fence, Parker saw that Chet was right on two counts: more weeds had sprouted overnight, and there weren't as many as the day before.

"Get pulling?" asked Chet.

"Get pulling," confirmed Parker.

The boys crouched in separate rows and went to work. Parker wasn't moving as quickly as Chet, but he was faster than the day before. Pulling left hand, right hand, left hand, right hand, weeds tossed into the bucket, and then moving the bucket a few paces forward.

Parker cringed each time his hands wrapped around a weed.

Chet glanced over sympathetically.

"Just try not to think about it, man."

"Thanks for the tip." Parker winced.

The sun continued to rise. The day warmed. Parker's body found new ways to ache. And he did his best to think about anything other than the pain. Sadly, that was easier said than done.

But before Parker knew it, they had finished the

field's first pen and were hopping a fence to the second. Unfortunately for Parker, as they moved through the day, each pen became more challenging than the last. Even with the gloves, it felt like his hands were on fire. And it was like someone had kicked his back and punched his shoulders. Things were miserable.

Then Parker's boot got stuck in something and he toppled over.

"You okay, man?" asked Chet, helping him up. "Snake hole."

Parker brushed himself off. It was a pointless exercise, since he was plastered in dirt already. He looked back at the boot-sized opening in the ground that he'd tripped on. "Snake hole?"

"Yeah, man. Snakes don't really dig, but they take over the homes of gophers and stuff and make the openings bigger. That's why your boot got stuck."

"Like garter snakes?"

"One that size? Probably a rattler."

Parker went white. "There are rattlesnakes crawling around out here?"

Chet frowned. "Snakes don't crawl, man, they slither."

"You know what I mean, Chet. Is there a rattlesnake in these radishes?"

"Probably not now. They usually become nocturnal in the summer because it's so hot."

"Usually?"

"Usually. We'll tell Mingo where the burrow is and he can take care of it."

"He'll kill it?"

Chet shrugged. "I doubt he'll find the snake. But if he gets rid of all of the places it can hide, eventually it'll move to a different farm."

"Eventually?"

"Maybe."

Parker's skin squirmed as he glared at the snake hole. "We should probably move away from here as quickly as possible, right?"

"I'd say so, man."

The guys pulled double-time until they'd gotten far enough away from the burrow.

Parker peered at the other boys across the farm. They seemed to be working on—well, he wasn't sure. Was it a radio tower? A jungle gym?

A metal pyramid sat on four humongous tires, with a pole on top leading to another pyramid on four more tires. It stood nearly ten feet tall and was at least thirty feet long. He knew that from across the field because when Carlos sat on Tyrone's shoulders and reached up with a wrench, he could barely touch the top pole between the pyramids. Walter busied himself with an issue with the tires.

Curiosity got the best of Parker. "What is that thing?" he panted out.

Chet glanced across the field. "That's how we're going to get Wednesday and Friday afternoons off, man. New irrigation system. Supposed to take half the time to water the field that it used to."

Parker nodded. Sounded good to him.

That day Parker and Chet stopped for lunch.

Technically it wasn't a break, because they didn't eat with Mingo, Molly, and the boys. Not wanting the afternoon to get away from them, they grabbed their food and headed back into the field.

Never in his life would Parker have thought that an egg salad sandwich could bring him so much joy.

9

PARKER AND CHET returned their buckets and gloves to the supply shed and rolled into the barn six minutes before dinner. The boys were covered in dirt, and Parker's knees hurt when they bent.

Tyrone peered up from a purple book titled *Farming, Physics, and the Secrets of the Universe*. His long legs nearly reached the end of his cot. "You made it!"

"And before dinner," Carlos said from behind a family-size bag of potato chips at the round table. He wiped crumbs off his cheeks.

Parker and Chet smiled and made their way to the sinks to wash up. "I don't know if I'm more tired or hungry," said Parker. "But I'm pretty sure there aren't any other places for my hands to sting."

"I used to despise pulling weeds," said Tyrone. "Who would have imagined that a person could get a paper cut from a plant?"

Parker gaped at his hands in the sink's lukewarm water. "Paper cuts. That's exactly what they feel like."

"They'll get better," said Carlos.

"Time heals all wounds," confirmed Tyrone, twirling a lock of his curly hair.

"How's the rig coming?" asked Chet.

"We're in for an easy Wednesday afternoon," said Carlos.

"Rejoice, rejoice my fellow workers," said Tyrone. "We shall rise from the soil and reign as lords of this ramshackle kingdom."

Parker smiled and shook his head. "How long have you guys known each other?"

"Since we were five," said Carlos.

"We met at the Future Farmers of Idaho Eight-and-Under Carrot Competition," said Tyrone. "Not only did we beat the older entrants, we *tied*. We had identical carrots. The odds of that happening are astronomical."

"Astronomical?" asked Parker.

"It'd be like getting three prizes in the same box

of cereal," said Carlos. "The judges couldn't believe it. Even we couldn't tell the carrots apart."

Parker frowned. "Don't they all kind of look the same?"

"You've clearly never closely examined a carrot," laughed Tyrone.

"I guess not," said Parker.

"Yeah, vegetables, they're like, um, fingerprints? They're all different. Carrots, Brussels sprouts, even radishes," said Carlos.

"It was like the world proclaimed that we needed to be best friends," said Tyrone.

Carlos popped another chip into his mouth. "Hard to win an argument against the whole world."

"Eventually we're starting a farm together," said Tyrone.

"Can't wait," said Carlos. "I'm going to be the first one in my family to have my own farm."

"Well, co-own," Tyrone said with a smile.

"Hold on," said Parker. "You two came all the way from Idaho?"

Tyrone shrugged. "Not many farms offer minors full-time employment opportunities with room and board. When Boss reached out, we leapt at the chance."

"He read in the newspaper about us sweeping the

entire growing competition a few years ago. We've been coming ever since."

Parker's lips twisted. "His paper had an article about a kids' farming contest a thousand miles away?"

"A sweep was unprecedented," said Tyrone.

Parker washed his elbows. It sounded strange, but maybe it was a slow news day. "You guys legitimately love farming, don't you?"

"Working the earth to make food come out? What could be more magical?" said Carlos.

Parker nodded. He'd never thought about it that way.

"Baa!" A goat's bleat echoed from the corral.

Parker felt his skin tingle. He glanced up from the sink. "Déjà vu."

"Hmm?" Tyrone asked from behind his book.

"Oh, nothing. I had a dream that I saw a flying goat....I actually got goose bumps just now. It's dumb, but have you ever had a dream that seemed completely real?"

Carlos pulled another fistful of chips from his bag. "Probably wasn't a dream."

Tyrone chuckled and shook his head.

"What do you mean?" Parker lathered his arms with soap.

"He's just being ridiculous," said Tyrone. "Tell him, Chet."

Chet scrubbed the dirt beneath his fingernails. "I'm staying out of it, man."

"I saw him," Carlos said through chews.

"Be rational, my friend," said Tyrone. "Please use your head."

"I saw what I saw," said Carlos. "Have to trust my heart. And my eyes."

"Saw what?" said Parker.

"The falling man," said Carlos.

"The who?"

Tyrone let out a heavy sigh. "Can we change the subject? It's a nice evening and if Walter hears this silly story again he's going to explode."

"It's not silly," said Carlos.

"What's that guy's deal?" asked Parker.

"Walter?" said Chet. "Well, he goes to some fancy boarding school, and has this big trust fund—"

Tyrone and Carlos waved their hands, miming for Chet to be quiet. Sadly, because Parker was drying his face with a hand towel, he missed the warnings.

"Trust fund? I mean, what's his problem? He's been such a—"

Parker stopped talking as he heard a toilet flush.

He lowered the hand towel and stared at the bathroom door with dread. Time slowed down.

The bathroom door opened and Walter stepped out. He clenched his fists and began crossing the room.

Tyrone went back to his physics book, Carlos busied himself with his chips, and Chet began drying off.

"Such a what?" Walter approached and towered over Parker.

Parker swallowed. "Such a patient person to wait for me to pull my foot out of my mouth?"

"I don't like you."

Parker nodded. "That's becoming more and more clear."

"I don't know why my aunt thinks you're even a little bit interesting. Or why she'd think we'd be good influences on each other. Or would ever be friends."

"Your aunt?"

"Eleanor Birdseye."

"Ms. Birdseye is your aunt?" Parker felt a cramp form in his stomach. "Wait. You're the rusty shovel!"

"The what?"

Parker's eyebrows raised as a realization hit. "Are you jealous of me because your aunt likes me?"

"You're going to be jealous of my fist in your face in a second."

Parker frowned. "That doesn't really make sense."

Walter stared down his nose at Parker. "I think you'll figure it out."

Tyrone, Carlos, and Chet watched to see what would happen next.

Parker bit his lip.

Clang, clang!

The dinner bell rang, and Mingo's voice echoed from outside. "Dinner under the stars tonight, fellas! Come on!"

Walter shook his head. "Let's go," he announced to the room. He bumped Parker with his shoulder as he made his way to the door.

Sore already, Parker winced but did his best to hide it. Everyone saw.

10

ON WEDNESDAY MORNING Parker was awoken by a punch to the ribs.

Walter stood over him. "Wake up."

"Ow." Parker rubbed his side. Looked around to find the other boys walking out the door. "Should I be setting an alarm or something?"

"You should stop sleeping in. Everyone needs to pull their weight today. Get moving." Walter kicked a cot leg, which caused the bed to collapse and Parker to spill onto the floor.

"I guess I'll get up," Parker mumbled from the ground as the larger boy headed for the exit.

Parker had spent most of the night worrying that

his relationship with Walter might negatively affect his friendship with Ms. Birdseye. Perhaps even his school tuition and his father's employment. Sure, Ms. Birdseye almost considered Parker like family, but Walter *was* family. Parker regretted his stunt at the pool more each day. Not only because working at the Leisure Centre would have been a vacation compared to the farm, but because he had let Ms. Birdseye down. She'd tried to do a nice thing, and in return, he'd embarrassed her. He wished he could do it over. Also, he wished Walter would stop hurting him.

He quickly got dressed and found Chet waiting outside. The sun was rising and the picnic table was empty.

Parker frowned. "Are we doing breakfast this morning?"

"Later, man." Chet nodded at the others, who were standing across the field around the new irrigation system. "We have to start watering before it gets too hot. We won't waste as much water and it'll take less time."

Parker's stomach growled as he took another look at the picnic table. Then he spotted Molly walking up the road toward the farm. "Where do you think she's coming from?"

"Delivery probably."

"On foot?"

"Local folks need radishes, too, man."

Parker watched Molly. "Lugging a crate of radishes across town wouldn't be my favorite way to start the day."

"Crate? Nah, man. Local deliveries are small. Usually only two or three radishes."

"Two or three? Like for an appetizer?"

"I don't know, man. I don't place the orders, I just work here."

"But doesn't that sound strange to you? Like, how does delivering two radishes make any sense?"

"Well, sometimes it's three."

"That doesn't really make it better."

Chet shrugged. "It's fifty percent more, man."

"But how would that make a delivery worthwhile?"

"They probably pay a premium."

Parker sighed. "It's at least unusual, right? Delivering only two or three radishes? Can we agree on that? That it seems like an odd waste of time?"

"Not really any of my business how Molly and Boss spend their days."

Parker stared at Chet. "This seriously doesn't bother you at all, does it?"

"No. We should get moving. Come on." Chet started toward the new machine.

Parker glanced at Molly again before jogging after Chet.

"So, what is that thing exactly?" asked Parker. "A big sprinkler?"

"Basically. It waters twelve rows of radishes at once. We just have to guide it along."

"What did you do before?"

"We used the longest hose you've ever seen. It took all day. We had to spread out across the field to hold the hose up and keep it from dragging across the ground and uprooting the radishes."

"Yeah?"

"Yeah. You think weed-pulling is bad? That was awful, man. The hose didn't weigh that much, but—How can I describe it? You know how the longer you hold a bushel of acorns the heavier it gets?"

"Sure, who doesn't?" said Parker.

"Now imagine holding twenty pounds of hose for eight hours. We could barely move the next day, man."

"Rough."

"Rough," confirmed Chet. "With this new thing, the hose screws in about nine feet off the ground and comes down gradually, so only one of us needs to keep it from dragging across the field. Two of us walk alongside the pyramids keeping it straight, while the other

82

guys take a break. We can rotate. And all of it in a third the time."

Parker admired the jungle-gym-looking sprinkler as they approached. "This feels like a much better system."

"Yep," said Chet.

Carlos sat on Tyrone's shoulders screwing the hose into the bar between the tops of the pyramids. Walter finished a last-minute adjustment to one of the wheels with Mingo, who had his hair up in a bun. Then Mingo popped up, helped Carlos down, and addressed the boys:

"Listen, fellas, let's take it nice and easy this morning. We need to be careful. This is a big piece of machinery and it can be dangerous if we're not paying attention. That said, this isn't rocket science, and if everyone stays focused, we can finish before lunch."

The boys nodded. Carlos and Tyrone clapped.

"Okay," continued Mingo. "Let's get ready to water the first pen. Walter, you're on hose duty. Tyrone and Carlos, you guys guide. Chet, can you get the spigot? Parker, why don't you start off watching with me?"

Parker stood next to Mingo as Tyrone and Carlos moved to the outsides of the pyramids. Walter stood about fifty feet back holding the hose off the field. Chet took the hose behind Walter and attached it to a spigot sprouting from the ground.

"All right, boys, rev it up," said Mingo. Carlos and Tyrone yanked the starter ropes on the lawn mower engines at the base of each pyramid. The motors rumbled to life.

"Wow, didn't even notice those," muttered Parker as the massive wheels beneath the pyramids slowly rolled forward.

Carlos and Tyrone guided the watering system through an opening in the fence of the nearest pen, then carefully lined up the wheels between rows of radishes.

"Do it, Chet!" called Mingo.

Chet turned the knob on the spigot. The hose wiggled, then went straight. A second later, water began sprinkling from the top bar onto twelve rows of crops below. It worked!

Mingo and the boys beamed as the machine rolled ahead, watering as it went.

Parker gave an approving nod. "Kind of genius."

Mingo nudged Parker and pointed to Molly, who had snuck out to the far corner of the pen and taken a seat on the blue fence. "Molly invented it."

"Seriously?"

Mingo nodded. "Yeah, I helped a little with the welding, but it was all her."

Parker watched as Molly admired her invention efficiently watering the field.

"Not bad, right?" asked Mingo.

"Not bad at all," said Parker.

After the machine completed its slow journey spraying the left side of the pen, Carlos, Tyrone, and Walter began carefully realigning its wheels to water the right side. Parker took the changeover as an opportunity to visit Molly. Her head was buried in a notebook.

Parker drummed his fingers on the fence. "What are those motors, about twenty-four horsepower apiece?"

Molly snapped her book shut and examined Parker from her perch. "You know your engines."

"I have a stationary workout bike in my living room."

Molly snorted.

"Hey, you laughed," he said.

"I did. That was a stupid joke."

"Still counts. My dad is a mechanic. Motors are kind of in my blood." Parker nodded at Molly's watering rig. "That thing is cool."

"I like to fix the problems that I can."

"Not sure I could have figured out how to design something like that in a million years."

"You don't strike me as the type of person who puts in the effort to figure things out."

"Ouch."

"Maybe that's not fair. I'm not saying you're not smart. Just that you're self-centered and lazy."

Parker laughed. "How is that better?"

Molly pushed a strand of hair behind her ear as she weighed his question. "It's probably not."

"You don't really know me," he said.

"But I can always spot your type right away. Tell me I'm wrong to think that you're usually the only kid in class who doesn't do the homework."

"Sure, but that doesn't mean I don't put in the effort. Like, let's say everybody else spends fifteen to forty-three minutes doing a math assignment after school? It might take me the *whole day* to convince the teacher that I should be excused because my neighbor's guinea pig is sick."

Molly hopped off the fence as the boys finished turning the machine around. "That sounds like a ridiculous waste of your time and your teacher's when you say it out loud, doesn't it?"

Parker opened his mouth to respond, but his face fell as he caught himself. "I guess it kind of does."

He thought for a moment. "Hey, speaking of wastes of time, is it true that you delivered two radishes to someone this morning?"

Molly made a line in the soil with a boot. "None of our deliveries are a waste of time."

"So, it's not true?"

"We only deliver what people need."

"What does that mean?"

"Exactly what it sounds like."

Parker twisted his lips as Molly headed toward the others.

"You can understand why I might be confused, though, right? Delivering only two radishes sounds strange."

"Embrace the extraordinary," she called over her shoulder.

"Are you just messing with me now?"

"Might be. Could go either way."

Parker smiled and jumped off the fence.

11

MOLLY AND THE boys sat cross-legged in the field during breakfast. Plates of grits and toast in front of them and wispy clouds in the sky. Radish leaves swayed in the breeze. Parker twirled a weed between his fingers. "So what's the falling man story, Carlos?"

"Ugh. Don't humor him," said Walter.

Carlos perked up. "I've been waiting for you to ask."

"You're always waiting for someone to ask," said Walter.

Carlos ignored Walter. "It's weird, today is just like the day I saw him. Fell straight through clouds like those."

Parker stopped twirling the weed and stared at Carlos. "Saw what, now?"

Walter rolled his eyes.

"My colleague believes he witnessed a gentleman plummet through the stratosphere last summer," said Tyrone.

"Hold on. Your falling man story is actually about a *falling man*?" asked Parker.

"What else would it be about?" said Chet.

"Dropped right from the sky," said Carlos through chews. "Like he jumped out of an airplane, but there wasn't an airplane? Like an angel that lost his wings."

"Yeah right," said Parker. He looked to Molly for validation, but she was focused on her food.

"It happened," said Carlos. "I was pulling weeds over there when I heard the loudest scream of my life. I thought Boss was being chased by a pack of bears or something, right? I didn't even think to look up at first. But then I saw this old guy yelling and falling toward that pen. Like twenty yards from me? I shut my eyes right before he hit and waited for the splat, but then there wasn't a sound. And when I opened my eyes there wasn't a body, either."

Parker's forehead wrinkled.

"There wasn't a body because there wasn't a guy in the first place," said Walter. "You were daydreaming."

"I saw what I saw."

"You should get your eyes checked," said Walter.

Carlos shook his head. "Nah. It happened. And the scream is the thing I'll never forget. I still can't believe no one came outside. The guy was shrieking his head off. And he was going to crash into that field right there. He was close enough for me to see his bushy gray mustache wiggling in the wind. But he just—I don't know. Disappeared?"

Parker watched Carlos stare at the field.

"Do you know how dumb you sound?" Walter asked.

"I don't care if you believe me."

"Molly, tell him how dumb he sounds," said Walter.

"You guys don't need to open your mouths to come across as dumb," said Molly. "But I believe you, Carlos." She stood and gave him a wink. Carlos smiled as Molly walked toward the irrigation machine.

"Ugh. Enough story time," said Walter. "Let's get back to it." Walter followed Molly.

Tyrone climbed to his feet and gave Carlos a hand. "I wish I could come up with a logical explanation for what you saw."

"Who says everything needs to be logical?" asked Carlos.

"The laws of physics," said Tyrone.

Parker watched the boys follow the others, then turned to Chet. "Carlos is serious about all that?"

"He thinks so, man," said Chet. "I guess maybe don't forget to look up every once in a while?"

Parker tried to get a read on Chet, but the shorter boy just stood. "We should get back to work, man."

Chet grabbed his plate. Parker gazed at the sky.

— ⁓ —

"Last pen, fellas," Mingo announced a few hours later. "Let's finish strong so we can relax before dinner."

The boys wiped away sweat, rolled their flannel sleeves higher. The sun was working overtime.

The irrigation system's wheels were aligned between the rows of radishes. Parker had spent most of the day holding the hose off the ground. He would finally be given a break by guiding the machine.

"It's not too challenging," explained Tyrone. "You just pull the rope to start the engine, then keep a steady hand on the bar to keep it running straight."

Carlos slapped Parker on the back. "You'll be fine. Just keep it steady, you know?"

Parker nodded. "Got it. Thanks, guys." He'd been

watching the last few hours. He figured he could do it in his sleep at this point.

"Nice and easy," said Mingo. "Don't overdo it, bud."

"I don't think we'll ever have to worry about Parker overdoing anything," Molly said, leaning against the blue fence. Parker grinned.

"Start it up, fellas!" called Mingo.

Chet and Parker pulled the ropes and the engines rattled to life. Carlos turned on a spigot and the bar began spraying water onto the radishes below.

Tyrone was on hose duty. Walter and Mingo took seats on the fence as the machine inched along. And Molly was once again buried in her notebook.

"Nice, Parker," called Carlos.

Tyrone gave an encouraging salute.

Parker smiled back before staring straight ahead. They only needed to go about a hundred yards, carefully turn the machine to spray the left half of the field, and then they would be done for the day. It should only take about forty minutes. Maybe fifty? This was definitely easier than pulling weeds, but time seemed to creep slower.

He wished the machine moved quicker but could

only imagine how much faster it was than having to water the field with a hose. Soon they could take the rest of the afternoon off.

Water from the machine spritzed Parker as he walked alongside his pyramid. It felt good in the sun. It was like being outside a restaurant with one of those misting systems under its awning.

He wondered what he would do that afternoon. Wondered what the other boys did with their free time. Carlos and Tyrone seemed nice. And he already liked Chet. Maybe now that he was beginning to get along with the others his summer wouldn't be so bad. Parker squinted through sunshine at the farmhouse's third story. Wondered if Molly's room was up there. Was that her window on the left? Maybe it was the Farmer's.

Was it hotter than yesterday? It felt hotter than yesterday.

He peered at the sky. Blue as far as he could see. And not a single gentleman screaming his head off. Parker glanced at Carlos. Shook his head. Poor guy must have been dizzy from dehydration.

He wondered how many summers Molly had been coming to the farm. Probably her entire life, right? He thought the two of them had an interesting dynamic.

He hoped she thought so, too. He should ask her about going on a walk to town sometime. Maybe he should confirm with someone that walking to town was even possible. It might be too far. He remembered their trek from the train station. And how he dripped with sweat. How his feet hurt. Looking back, that was his easiest morning since stepping off the train. In the short time he'd been on the farm, he'd decided that manual labor wasn't for him. He always imagined he'd grow up to work in an office. Not with his hands. It was one of the countless ways he thought he was less like his father and more like his—

"Hey, man!"

"Parker! What are you doing?"

"Whoa! *Stop!*"

Parker shook himself from his daydreams. Saw the upset faces around him. Felt something unexpected beneath his feet. Looked down to see he was standing on a clump of radishes. His pyramid's gigantic tires had rolled across five rows of plants, demolishing and uprooting everything in their path. It was like Parker had driven a semitruck through the field.

"Unbelievable," said Walter from his perch on the blue fence.

"What happened, bud?" asked Mingo, hurrying over.

Parker tried to assess the situation. "I don't know. I think—I guess I zoned out a little?"

Mingo turned off the engine and sighed. "Look at this mess." Radishes were everywhere. The rows weren't exactly rows anymore. Water continued to spritz down on them. "You did a real number on this field." He turned to Tyrone and Carlos. "Can one of you get that spigot?"

The water stopped and the other boys kicked their

boots into the dirt and mud, mumbled under their breaths.

Then Parker noticed Molly, hunched over with her hands on her knees. He watched her shoulders heave. Was she having a panic attack? He wondered why she was taking it so hard.

"Parker."

He turned to a stern-faced Mingo. Took a step back and threw up his hands. "I mean, it wasn't all me. Chet, didn't you see anything?"

Chet reacted like Parker had punched him in the stomach. "My engine ran out of gas. I called you, man. You were just gazing off at nothing."

Parker looked at the rows next to Chet. They were fine. Chet's wheels had stayed clear of the radishes while Parker's pyramid had curved across rows of crops.

"How hard is this, Big City?" said Walter. "You just had to walk in a straight line! So much for an early day..."

"Yeah, sorry, fellas," said Mingo, surveying the damage. "Better grab the gear from the supply shed. I'll let Boss know we're having a late dinner. This is going to take a while to fix."

The other boys groaned. But Parker shrugged. "Can't we do it tomorrow?"

Mingo inspected the demolished beds. "They won't be salvageable if they're out of the soil overnight."

"But why does that matter?" pressed Parker. "I'm tired. I need a break. I'm sure everyone else does, too."

"We're here to take care of the crops," said Mingo.

"Yeah. And thanks for ruining everything for everyone," said Walter. "Why finish early when we can work late? Big help, Big City."

Parker's lips parted, but no words came out.

Carlos rolled his eyes. Tyrone shook his head, squatted to examine the field.

Parker felt hot and itchy. But mostly annoyed with himself for making such a mess. And annoyed with the others for not shrugging it off. Half of him wanted to crawl into a hole. The other half wanted to explode. There had to be a way to get them to see that this wasn't a big deal.

"Come on, what are we even doing?" said Parker. "They're only radishes. People eat around them in salads. Who cares? All of this is just busywork. It's not like these are life skills that I need or anything. I shouldn't even be here. I'm not gonna grow up and dig ditches."

Molly's eyes went wide.

Chet exhaled and studied his boots.

Walter crossed his arms.

Carlos's head snapped back. "You think you're too good for farmwork?"

"I had no idea that we've been rubbing shoulders with royalty," said Tyrone.

"That came out wrong," Parker said. "But you guys know what I mean."

"Know what you mean? Nah, it sounds like we're too simpleminded to understand, Big City. Why don't you explain it to us slowly?" said Walter.

"I'm just saying we shouldn't have to do this," mumbled Parker.

"It's our job, bud," said Mingo. "And it's your mess, but we're all going to fix it together."

The other boys stared daggers at Parker.

Molly shook her head, then rested it on the fence.

12

IT TOOK THE boys three hours to rebuild the smashed radish beds. Then with Molly's help, another hour to safely maneuver the irrigation system into position to water the rest of that final pen. Parker was forced to resume hose duty.

No one spoke to Parker that afternoon other than an occasional curt instruction. When they finished, the radish beds looked good as new. Mingo and Molly returned her machine to the far side of the farmhouse. The other boys slapped backs and hands, but Parker was left hanging.

Parker figured it would blow over by dinner. That was how his fights with Kevin worked back home.

One of them would say something they didn't mean. The other would steam for a couple of hours, and then they'd forget all about it. He thought this would be like that.

He was wrong.

As the other boys joked and ate at the picnic table under the moonlight, Parker approached and began to take a seat.

"Whoa," said Walter. "We're kind of having a private conversation, Big City."

Parker stood up straight. Smiled. "Well, do you mind if I just eat here at the end of the table quietly?"

"We do mind," said Walter.

Parker's smile faded. He looked to the other boys for help. Tyrone chewed his burger. Carlos frowned and shrugged. And Chet stared at his food.

"Well, where should I eat?" Parker asked.

"We don't really care," Walter said. "Why don't you take a walk?"

Parker scanned the table again for help. Tyrone, Carlos, and Chet wouldn't make eye contact, but Walter never broke his off.

So Parker nodded and wandered toward the field with a plate as the joking and laughter resumed behind his back. As he drifted away from the group, he wrestled with the idea that for the first time in his life, people didn't like him. It felt awful. Then it occurred to him that this was probably only the first time he was aware of, which felt worse.

He walked to the farthest pen, put his plate on a post, and sat on the railing. He reasoned that some time apart would be good for everyone. Even him. He could get his head straight. It was a concept that his father had suggested to him numerous times, but he'd never tried it. Visualize how he wanted things to be, and then work toward that goal. But all Parker could think about was how bad it felt to be shunned, unwelcomed, and disliked.

He gazed at the blanket of stars covering the sky. He could see so many more on the farm than in Pittsburgh. But rather than appreciating their beauty, it made him feel small.

He heard the faint ringing of a bicycle bell as Mingo pedaled up the dirt road to the barn from a night on the town.

He watched as Mingo and the boys headed inside.

Then Parker watched and waited some more.

When it became too cold to sit any longer, Parker hopped off the fence and made the lonely walk to the barn. The others had passed out by the time he got inside.

Parker climbed into bed and stared at the ceiling.

He was mad at himself for behaving so poorly. Then he was upset with his father for sending him to the farm in the first place. Which led him to resenting his mother for not being around, and when he decided that was unfair, he felt worse for thinking it at all. He steamed for an hour before falling asleep.

He was awoken sometime later when his head dropped to the cot with a thud. His pillow had been pulled from under his head. Parker looked up to see Walter standing over him, ripping his blanket away as well.

Walter brought a finger to his lips, then returned to his cot, putting Parker's things under his own pillow and going back to sleep.

Parker Kelbrook was cold and alone. He turned toward the wall and quietly cried.

⁓

Parker woke at dawn the next day. He pulled on a flannel and overalls, rolled up his sleeves and cuffs, and crept from the barn while the others slept.

The grass was covered in dew. Hints of sunlight were beginning to sneak over the corn-lined horizon. Parker took a breath of crisp morning air, shoved his hands in his pockets, and began a walk around the field.

He and Kevin used to spend hours strolling through the city. Running into kids they knew. Meeting others. Exploring. Procrastinating. Talking. He missed Kevin. He missed sidewalks. He missed Pittsburgh.

He wondered how Kevin liked that job at the surf shop. Wondered if he'd gotten tan at the beach. That was certainly one of the silver linings of working on the farm. Parker was getting plenty of sun. Sure, it was a farmer's tan, with all the color going to his face, neck, hands, and forearms, but that seemed to be the norm here.

Parker stopped as he circled the pen closest to the farmhouse. Did something move in the corn along the property line?

He looked closer.

Then something stepped from the cornfield.

A mangy dog. Perhaps part terrier, certainly a mutt. Its curly black fur was encrusted with years of dirt. The dog panted. Took a seat and tilted its head at Parker.

Parker looked like he'd witnessed Bigfoot emerging.

The dog raised a paw.

"You didn't strike me as an early riser."

Parker turned to see Molly in jeans and a jacket making her way back from a walk of her own. Her hair up, and her notebook in hand.

"Didn't sleep that well," he admitted.

"Domestic squabbles?"

"That's fair to say."

"You made quite the mess yesterday."

"Occasionally I color outside the lines and say the wrong things."

"I thought you said people tended to like you."

Parker shrugged. "I was mistaken."

"Clearly. Maybe just give it some time."

"Maybe," he said.

"And maybe keep your head down and put the work in."

Parker sighed. "I suppose there might be something to that, too."

"There's something to everything I say," she said.

Parker smiled.

Molly nodded and headed to the farmhouse.

Parker watched her go before looking back toward the property line. The dog was gone.

He sighed, got his bucket and gloves, and started pulling weeds.

Parker had finished two pens by the time Chet grabbed a bucket. He watched hopefully as Chet walked his way. He waited for some kind of acknowledgment or sign of appreciation for getting an early start. But nothing came. Instead, Parker was crushed more than he thought possible when the skinny boy started pulling weeds in a separate pen. Parker tried to shake the slight, but it stung. And so did his hands as he continued pulling weeds.

He was excluded during the meals that day, too. Sure, he was allowed to eat with the others, but all of his questions, comments, and jokes were ignored. And shortly after he dropped into bed that evening, his pillow and blanket were stolen again.

Things continued like that over the next few days. Parker would wake before the sun and go for a walk. Those early walks became the highlights of his days. He could think clearly and no one was mad at him yet.

Sometimes he would see Molly returning from one of her odd local deliveries, but her head was usually buried in her notebook, so he couldn't catch her attention.

After the walks, Parker got a head start on the day's chores, for himself and the others. He would work through aches and pains until whatever he was asked to do was completed. But the other boys kept ignoring him. And Walter kept stealing his bedding.

Parker's hands began to feel better over time. They still looked awful, but they didn't sting whenever he pulled a weed, which allowed him to move faster. He kept his head down and his emotions bottled up and focused on his work.

After his pillow was yanked for the seventh night in a row, Parker realized that the thefts bothered him less and less. As he stared at the ceiling while the others drifted to sleep, he questioned if, with enough time, it wouldn't bother him at all. If he would become numb to it. Whether he could make himself numb to anything and everything. It was a concept he found soothing and distressing.

There were certain things he wasn't sure he'd ever want to *get over*. Thoughts he didn't want to let go of. Pain he didn't want to forget. Happy memories that made him sad, that he wouldn't trade for the world. But perhaps things would be better if he could.

He could be more like the kid he used to be.

Someone driven.

Someone who took things seriously.

Less like the person who got himself sent to the

farm in the first place. Though he had to admit, he was getting better at dealing with the farm's curveballs. Sure, the others weren't accepting him, but at least he was figuring out how to navigate this place. Learning what to expect. Becoming less surprised by the things that happened there. And as he began to take comfort in that thought, he looked out the window and saw a dozen puffy flecks of white twirling beyond the glass.

Parker's mouth hung as he attempted to process the enchantment outside.

Snow in the middle of summer?

How?

He blinked. His vision remained unchanged.

Overtaken by curiosity, he slipped on a pair of jeans and boots and crept into the night. There he discovered thousands of tiny puffs zipping through the air. Diving up and down and across the farm. Like fairies bathing beneath the starlight. Parker smiled as he tried to make sense of the miracle. There wasn't snow on the ground. Perhaps it was something else? What could it be?

He held out a hand. Waited until a piece of fluff settled into his palm.

It wasn't wet.

Or cold.

It felt weightless.

He brought it closer, but as he did the fuzz blew away.

He wanted to get his bunkmates. To share the spectacle and see if they could make sense of it. But then he worried they would just be annoyed with him for waking them.

"You should be in bed."

Parker turned to find the Farmer sitting at the picnic table, watching the particles in the air.

"It sheds every other year," continued the Farmer, "and even then, we're lucky if it blows our way for a few hours."

Parker watched the spiraling wisps. "What is it?"

"Cottonwood. There's an orchard about three miles from here. When the wind hits it just right, it'll carry the cotton all the way to town."

Parker's eyes narrowed at the strands of cotton sailing across the field. "It feels like a dream," he said.

The Farmer grunted his agreement.

They admired the wondrousness.

Parker grinned. "When I was little, I was one of those kids that constantly asked questions. Like, 'Why this,' 'Why that,' 'How come Grandpa's foot hurts,' you know? My mom always tried to give me answers, but obviously nobody knows everything. So when I asked something she didn't know, she'd say, 'Because it got sprinkled with moondust,' and I just accepted that. I used to imagine that moondust kind of looked like this."

He watched the Farmer watch the cotton.

The Farmer stood. "You're on a stronger path, Parker. Don't stray."

Parker frowned. "Path to what?"

The Farmer walked home instead of responding. So Parker watched the cotton awhile longer before going to bed.

The next day after breakfast, Chet decided to pull weeds with him in the same pen.

They didn't speak, but Parker couldn't remember the last time he was so happy.

13

WHEN PARKER RETURNED to the barn from his morning stroll on Friday, he found the other boys gone. Mingo glanced up from a magazine. "Hey, bud."

"Where is everyone?"

"They took the buggy to pick up fertilizer," he said with a turn of the page. "Probably won't be back for a couple of hours."

"Should I wait here for them?"

Mingo looked around the bunk. "You should probably just get to the weeds."

"Oh."

So Parker nodded and went to work.

He was halfway through his second pen when he heard the other boys hoot and holler from what he figured must be the buggy.

An open wagon with two wheels pulled by a couple of horses made its way up the dirt road to the farm. The buggy's bed was stacked high with bags of fertilizer. All four boys were crammed onto the bench up front.

Parker waved as they rode to the supply shed. He got a halfhearted hand raise from Chet but nothing from the others. He sighed and kicked himself internally as the others kicked him figuratively.

How long did they plan on being mad at him?

Why couldn't he have kept his mouth shut?

Worse, why did he think for a second that he was better than them? He figured they had a right to be upset. So Parker resumed doing the only thing he could think of to make amends: he pulled weeds while the other boys unloaded fertilizer.

Parker didn't look up again until he had started the third pen. By that point, the boys were laughing over lunch. Parker was starving, but he wasn't in the mood to be alone in a group. So he worked through the growls of his stomach.

Fortunately, when Parker moved to the final pen, Molly approached with a plate of food and a cup of water. "Your train is rolling back this afternoon. Mingo and I are going to grab what's left of your luggage."

"Thanks, but I've kind of fallen in love with the hand-me-downs. They're inspiring me to become a giant."

"You should eat. Why don't you take a break and join the other guys?"

Parker eyed the food. Thought maybe Molly's decision to carry it all the way over was a hint. "I think I'm going to push through and keep working."

"Suit yourself." Molly set the plate and cup on a fence post. "I'll put these here for when you're ready. Tuna casserole with cut-up pieces of bologna. Tastes better than it sounds."

"Thanks, Molly." He stood for a moment; he didn't want her to go, so he asked the first thing that came into his mind. "So, are you here the whole summer?" He cringed. It sounded silly to him as it left his lips. But then she said:

"I'm here for good."

Parker tilted his head. "What about Topeka?"

"What about it?"

"I thought you said that's where you're from."

"It is. But I've been here since my parents died."

"Oh. I'm sorry. I had no idea."

"I hadn't told you. Not really something I talk

about. But you kind of asked, and I kind of felt it was okay to say."

"Thanks for telling me."

Molly shrugged. "Everyone deals with loss. Just some of us more than most."

Parker nodded. Wondered if she expected him to share, too. But before he could, she switched gears.

"Are you planning on patching things up with the others, or are things going to stay uncomfortable around here?"

"I'm doing what you said. Keeping my head down and putting the work in."

"Did you apologize?"

"A little late for that, don't you think?"

Molly rolled her eyes. "It's never too late. You really have a lot to learn, Parker." And with that, she headed off to grab Mingo from the corral.

Parker sighed. Peeled off his work gloves and tossed them into his bucket. Then he climbed onto the fence and grabbed the plate.

The casserole didn't look appetizing. Gray, and equal parts chunky and slimy. But he was starving, so he closed his eyes, held his breath, and took a bite. It wasn't bad.

As he stuck his fork down for another mouthful, he heard a whimper. He glanced up.

Sitting off under the water tower was the mangy dog from the neighboring farm's cornfield.

"It's you."

The dog raised a paw.

Parker took another bite. The dog whimpered again.

"Hungry?" Parker asked through chews.

The dog stared back.

Parker glanced around. Peered into the corn along the property line. "Are you alone? I don't really have enough to share if you're part of a roving band of farm dogs or something."

The dog panted. Parker shrugged. Jumped from the fence and walked to the tower.

"It's just you, isn't it?"

The dog gingerly stepped toward Parker. The boy kneeled and used his fork to push half the casserole off his plate and onto the ground in front of the dog. The dog stared up at Parker.

"It's not bad. Look." Parker took another bite from his plate. That was all the motivation the dog needed to gobble the casserole on the ground in a single chomp.

"Wow, you're starving."

The dog panted.

Parker set his plate in front of the dog, who promptly licked up the rest of the casserole.

"Impressive. So, are you an outcast like me?"

The dog smiled. Parker stepped to the fence. Took a long drink from his water. Then he bent down, tilted the cup, and let the dog lap up the rest.

"Thirsty, too." Parker placed the empty cup and plate back on a fence post for later. Pulled on his gloves. "Well, that's all I got. See you later, Outcast."

Parker grabbed the bucket, climbed the fence, and began pulling the weeds from the final pen.

Then something moved out of the corner of Parker's eye. He looked up to see the dog sitting under the fence.

"I don't have anything else. You should get back into that cornfield and out of this heat."

Outcast's front paws inched forward as he lay down to get comfortable.

Parker sighed. "Okay, boy. I'll work quickly so we can get out of the sun."

The dog watched and Parker worked.

~

When Parker finished the fourth pen, he picked up his bucket and nodded at the dog. Outcast rose and trotted toward the cornfield, like he understood they were done for the day.

"Appreciate the support," Parker said as he wiped away sweat with the sleeve of his flannel.

After putting his things back in the supply shed, he found Chet washing up with the hose outside the barn.

"Thanks for all the help with the weeds, man," said Chet.

Parker's heart skipped. He was surprised by how good it felt to hear Chet talk to him. It seemed like ages since the others had thrown anything but insults in his direction. He took a breath, then nodded. "Figured it's the least I can do."

"I'll never get used to the smell of fertilizer," said Chet.

"New project?"

"We sprinkle fresh fertilizer over the field every few weeks. We're all doing it tomorrow."

Parker scratched his head. "I thought you said this place had good soil."

"That's probably a big reason why." Chet finished washing and handed Parker the hose with a smile. "It's barbecue night."

"Yeah?" Parker tried to scrub the dirt off his forearms.

"Boss's specialty. He only cooks a few times a summer."

"Will, um, Boss and Molly eat dinner with us tonight, or is that just breakfasts and lunches sometimes?"

"Why? Do you like Molly?"

Parker lost track of the hose in his hand for a moment and sprayed more water than he would have preferred into his face. He shut off the spigot. "Of course not—I mean, she's all right. I was only wondering."

"It's okay. Everyone kind of likes Molly, man. We're all kind of scared of her, too. Not exactly warm and fuzzy, right? But anyway, I don't think she's coming. She and Boss usually cover the phones at night."

Parker frowned. "Why do they need to cover the phones at night? Are they shipping these radishes internationally?"

Chet shrugged. "I don't know much about phones, man. My grandmother doesn't even have one. We don't know that many people. I just heard sometimes they get their most desperate calls at night."

Parker couldn't imagine someone desperately needing a radish, but then again, he didn't know much about the importing and exporting of root vegetables.

The boys went inside and found Walter pulling Parker's tweed sport coat from one of the newly delivered suitcases. "I thought I was rich, but you really are fancy, Big City!"

Parker's face fell as Walter tried on the jacket. The sleeves didn't quite reach the larger boy's wrists. "A little snug, but I feel ready to pull some weeds."

Carlos and Tyrone focused on their card game at the round table. Parker tried to control his breathing to stay calm.

Walter flipped through the contents of Parker's bags. "Look at this stuff. You only packed suits and jackets?"

Parker shrugged.

"Wait. Is this a tuxedo?" Walter lifted a burgundy tux.

"It was from my second cousin Helga's third wedding. You never know when you'll need one and rentals are expensive."

"Who brings this kind of stuff to work on a farm?"

Parker stared at the floor, a little embarrassed. "I didn't really know what I was getting into, but I've always kind of thought it feels good to look nice."

Walter fumbled through the suitcase and pulled out the framed photograph. "What do we have here?"

Parker felt his muscles tense.

"Who is this, Parker?" said Walter. "You have a secret older girlfriend? Or is this your mommy?"

Parker exhaled through his nose. Used every ounce of will to keep his composure. "Put it back, please."

Walter's eyes went wide as he smiled. "Oh, does someone miss his mommy?"

Carlos and Tyrone looked up from their cards. Chet scratched the back of his head, seemed uncomfortable.

Parker stared at Walter as his heart pounded.

"Who travels with a framed picture of their mom?" said Walter. "What's wrong with you?"

"Please," Parker said again.

Walter cocked the picture behind his head, ready to throw it against the wall.

"Please," Parker repeated.

Walter snorted. Tossed the frame onto the suitcase and shook his head. Parker's muscles relaxed.

"You really think you're better than everyone, don't you?" said Walter.

All eyes on Parker.

Parker took a deep breath. "No. I absolutely don't."

Walter peeled off the jacket in disgust. Dropped it to the floor. "Right."

"Look, I said some stupid things I didn't mean. I realize that, and I'm trying here. I want to pull my own weight. And I know I have to keep making it up to you guys."

Walter's jaw clenched. Tyrone and Carlos crossed their arms.

"So, anyway," Parker continued, "I'm sorry. Really. I was dumb, and I have a lot to learn here. From all of you. Seriously. I'm sorry."

His words hung in the room. Parker swallowed. Waited.

"Is that it?" asked Carlos.

"That's it," said Parker.

Tyrone nodded. "All right. Would you mind giving us a moment?"

Parker tried to read the room. The other boys only gave blank stares. "Sure," he said before shuffling out of the barn. No one said anything as he left.

Outside, Mingo was finishing setting the picnic table with silverware on red cloth napkins. Parker took a seat.

"Good work this week, bud."

"Thanks, Mingo."

"I'll grab dinner."

Parker nodded as Mingo left.

And then he waited.

He could hear some kind of discussion going on in the barn, but not what was being said. He couldn't even make out the tone of the conversation: whether it was good or bad.

So he sat some more.

The conversation inside stopped. Or at least got very, very quiet. Parker leaned forward. Stared at the barn door. Strained to hear anything.

And then the barn door opened and Chet stepped

out wearing Parker's tweed sport coat. Parker watched perplexed as Chet sat at the table, a serious look on the skinny boy's face.

Then Tyrone came out and took a seat wearing Parker's corduroy jacket. Parker couldn't have been more confused.

But then Parker smiled as Carlos exited wearing the burgundy tuxedo and took a seat. "You know what, Parker? You were right. It does feel good to look nice."

The boys busted up laughing. Parker thought he was going to float away, he was so relieved.

Walter came out last.

He didn't have on any of Parker's things but wore a scowl across his face.

Forty-five minutes later the red cloth napkins sat unused. The boys and Parker's clothes were covered in barbecue sauce, but Parker didn't mind in the slightest.

Barbecue night was absolutely the best meal Parker had eaten since leaving Pittsburgh. Plates and bowls of brisket, ribs, chicken, mac & cheese, corn, mashed potatoes, and biscuits were spread across the table, and smiles were all around. After delivering the food from the farmhouse's kitchen, Mingo rode his bicycle to town, allowing Parker and the guys to have a boys' dinner and further smooth things over.

"So, I get to the edge of the pond," laughed Carlos, "and I'm about to come out when I see that my clothes are gone!"

"Did they blow away in the wind?" Tyrone asked through a laugh.

"I wish! There was this frilly pink thing where I left them. Then I hear giggling and see my big sister and her friend ride away on their bikes!"

"No way!" said Walter.

"And what dare I ask was the pink thing?" said Tyrone.

"My sister's ballet tutu! I had to wear it the whole way home!" chuckled Carlos.

The table erupted with laughter. Parker shared a smile and a shake of the head with Carlos.

"Serves you right," said Tyrone. "Who goes skinny-dipping alone?"

"It was hot!" Carlos said with a laugh.

Parker and the boys laughed harder. Then Walter's face became serious. Angry even.

"Hey! Get out of here!" he yelled toward the field.

All eyes followed his to Outcast, who sat a dozen yards from the table.

"Go!" yelled Walter as he chucked a corncob at Outcast. The dog calmly watched as the cob sailed to his right.

"Whoa, easy," said Parker.

"Yeah, leave him alone," said Carlos.

Walter shook his head. "He's gonna dig holes every-where and make more work for us. He's like the animal version of Big City."

"He wouldn't do that," said Parker. "He's okay."

Walter snorted. "You're the last person I'd listen to about whether someone else was okay. Even a dog."

"He's a good dog," said Parker.

"He's a mutt," said Walter.

"He's a good mutt." Parker grabbed his plate and walked to Outcast.

"Ah, come on," said Walter. "If you feed him he'll never leave us alone."

The dog smiled as Parker placed the plate in front of him. He gobbled the remains of a roll and some mashed potatoes, then happily took a beef rib and scurried off.

Walter rolled his eyes. "Great...If that dog messes anything up around here, you have to fix it. He's your responsibility."

Parker grinned as Outcast scampered into the cornfield.

A screen door banged shut, which turned all eyes to the Farmer. He walked an old man with a bushy gray mustache from the farmhouse to a parked white pickup truck.

Carlos went pale. "No way."

"What?" said Parker.

"That's the man I saw fall from the sky."

14

THE BOYS HURLED whispers across their beds.

"It was just a guy who looks like a lot of people," said Walter. "Walk around any town for an afternoon and you'll find three old men with mustaches just like that."

"It wasn't just his mustache. It was *him*," whispered Carlos.

"Carlos," said Tyrone, "I'm not doubting what you believe you saw, but you have to admit, it's fairly dark out this evening and we were rather far away."

Parker watched as Carlos considered.

"I don't know," said Carlos. "I had a good look at him. At least I think I did."

"How sure are you?" asked Parker.

"Pretty sure," said Carlos.

"What do you think, Chet?" said Parker.

"Maybe it was. Maybe it wasn't," said Chet.

The boys frowned at Chet.

"Very helpful, Chet," said Walter.

"Just sharing my opinion, man."

The barn door creaked open and the whispers stopped as Mingo stepped in and promptly passed out on his cot. A half hour later, Walter tiptoed across the room and stole Parker's pillow and blanket. Parker didn't even have to be shushed anymore—he knew to keep his mouth shut. And knew that though the others were starting to like him again, Walter probably never would.

Parker couldn't wrap his head around how the farm could be so hot during the day and freezing at night—one of the great mysteries of summer in Midwestern America. And he couldn't stop thinking about the old man with the bushy mustache. He curled into a ball in an attempt to get warm. It would be difficult to sleep. The howling wind didn't help, but at least it was entertaining.

Parker watched through the front window as the neighboring farm's cornfield danced in the moonlit windstorm. He lost track of time as the stalks bent, twirled, rose and fell.

Then he was startled by a thump.

Did the barn just shake?

It sounded like the thud had come from above.

Had something crashed onto the roof? Or *someone*?

He stared up.

Waited for more.

Anything.

Maybe it was nothing?

He looked around the room.

The others slept as the wind shrieked. So he tried to sleep, too.

Then Parker was jolted by a *clomp-clomp-clomp-ding-ding*. And the sound seemed to be coming from the ceiling.

He strained to listen.

Even over the wailing wind he heard his heart beating in his chest.

He stared at the rafters. Had someone climbed up there to play a practical joke? He peered into the darkness but couldn't see anyone hiding in the support beams.

He looked to the far end of the room. Walter dozed with two pillows and two blankets.

Parker scrutinized the ceiling. Tried to control his breathing to stay calm.

Clomp-clomp-ding-ding.

Then Parker heard something new. Was that the sound of metal clanging?

The wind squealed, and the noise intensified. Parker watched as the other boys began waking with groans. Mingo started to snore.

"Ugh. What's that sound?"

"Make it stop so I can sleep."

As if on command, the banging stopped. But it was replaced by a new sound. A scratching. And it was close.

All eyes turned to the barn door.

Mingo's snoring kicked into overdrive.

The scratching got louder.

Tyrone asked exactly what Parker was thinking: "What is that?"

Parker stared at the door. He thought maybe if he looked hard enough, he might be able to see through it. Unfortunately, that didn't work.

The door began to shake.

Walter leapt from his bed.

"Are you going to open it?" asked Carlos.

"No way." Walter backed against the far wall. "Check it out, Big City."

Parker's eyes went wide. "Me? Why do I have to do it?"

"Because if you don't I'll pound you."

Scratch, scratch, scratch.

Parker looked from Walter to the door. Weighed his options: Outside it might only be the wind. Inside there would certainly be a pounding. He sighed and crept from his bed.

"Don't open it too quickly," said Tyrone.

"Yeah, and maybe not all the way, so you can still close it," suggested Carlos.

Parker frowned at the door as the scratching grew stronger. His heart raced. He inched toward the sound as the others retreated to the back wall.

Parker stared at the doorknob. Took a deep breath, then pulled it open. Outside he saw... nothing.

Just radish leaves rustling in the wind.

Then he felt something brush against his leg!

Parker jumped.

He looked down as Outcast pushed his way into the barn.

"Ah, don't let that mutt in here," whined Walter.

Tyrone let out a sigh of relief.

Carlos slapped Tyrone's back. "You were scared."

"So were you," said Tyrone as he climbed back into bed.

"I was," admitted Carlos.

Parker shut the door and smirked at the smiling dog.

Walter groaned. "I'm serious, Big City. Put him outside."

The dog looked questioningly at Parker. "But it's so cold out there," said Parker.

"He smells awful," said Walter.

"He's just wet," said Parker. "This is what wet dogs smell like."

"That dog has never had a bath in his life. Look at him. He's dripping mud."

"Let him stay, man," said Chet. "He's not gonna hurt anyone and he'll freeze in the wind."

Walter's upper lip curled. "You guys are nuts." He climbed under his pillows and blankets. "If he chews any of my stuff you're paying for it."

Parker gave an appreciative nod to Chet, who shrugged and got into bed.

Parker bent down and gave the muddy dog a rub on the head. Then got back on his cot and curled into a ball. It was still freezing even with his elevated blood pressure.

Then Outcast sprang onto the bed and cuddled up next to him. Dirt and all.

———

Parker woke early again the next morning and quietly dressed in the hand-me-downs (he had determined that nothing he packed was remotely practical for farm-work). He wiped up the muddy paw prints, threw his towel over his shoulder, and carried his cot out of the bunk. Outcast cheerfully followed at his heels.

The boy grabbed the hose on the side of the barn and sprayed down the dog and the bed. Outcast's black fur became a chocolate brown as a lifetime of grime washed away. Parker used his only towel to dry the dog and the cot.

Then the boy and his dog went for a walk around the farm.

When he passed the corral, he noticed that the gate was open. He closed it and scanned the field. It didn't appear that anything had gotten out. He figured the gate must have blown free in the wind. That must have been what he had heard clanging.

As he made his way back toward the barn, he saw

Molly strolling up the dirt road. Her notebook in the crook of an arm. He took a deep breath and waved. She looked quizzically at the dog, before delighting Parker with a wave back.

Then he heard a *clomp-clomp-clomp-clomp-ding.*

Outcast barked.

Parker gazed up and his mouth fell open.

On top of the barn was a seventeen-hundred-pound black-and-white dairy cow.

15

PARKER, THE DOG, and the boys stared slack-jawed at the cow on the roof.

"That's Martha all right," confirmed Carlos.

Martha took a couple of steps forward—*clomp, clomp*—and the bell around her neck rang—*ding, ding.* She peered down and gave an uneasy "Moo." Parker wondered if the cow was afraid of heights.

"Did she jump up there?" asked Chet.

Tyrone sighed. "Have you ever seen a cow jump?"

"I'm not sure. I want to say not that high?"

Walter sighed. "Cows don't jump, Chet. Don't be an idiot."

"You don't have to be mean about it, man. I was just asking. I'm not a cow doctor or anything."

The other boys shook their heads.

Tyrone turned to Parker. "She was up there when you returned from your walk?"

"Yeah. I think I heard her clomping around last night, too."

"Why didn't you say anything?" asked Walter.

"It didn't occur to me that there might be a cow on the roof," said Parker. "I probably would've guessed that Santa came in June first."

"Fair," said Tyrone.

"I just don't see how she could have gotten up there," mumbled Carlos.

"Maybe she fell out of an airplane with your buddy," said Walter.

"Leave me alone," said Carlos.

"Is there a ramp that leads to the roof?" asked Chet.

"Yeah, Chet," said Walter. "There's been an invisible ramp to the roof this whole time."

"There's an invisible ramp?"

Walter analyzed Chet. "I can't tell if you're messing with us or not."

The boys stared at the cow. The cow stared back. The dog panted happily.

Parker scratched his head. "So it's safe to assume that this kind of thing hasn't happened before?"

"At least not often," said Chet.

Mingo, Molly, and the Farmer approached with a long, thick spool of rope wrapped around their shoulders.

"All right, boys," said Molly. "Let's stop gawking and get the cow off the barn."

Parker watched from the ground as Mingo climbed out of the farmhouse's third-story window with the end of a rope wrapped around his shoulder and a power drill in one hand. The Farmer stepped out after him carrying the midsection of the rope. Molly hung her head out the window with the other end of the rope. "Center it six or so inches from the top," she said.

The Farmer and Mingo carefully navigated up the shingles and dropped their portions of rope next to the chimney.

Mingo reached into his back pocket and pulled out an iron hook about the size of a dinner plate and two fingers wide.

Parker looked on as Mingo used the drill to attach the hook to the top of the chimney with four heavy-duty screws from his flannel shirt's pocket. Then the Farmer threaded the rope over the hook.

"Done," called Mingo.

"Good," said Molly. "Stand clear!" Molly heaved her end of rope out the window. It landed on the ground with a thud. "Let's hook 'em up."

Parker picked up the rope, but Walter snatched it away. "Let me do it," Walter said. "It has to be tight." Parker put his hands up and moved out of the way as Walter tied the rope to the back of the buggy, which had the horses hitched up front.

Then Parker held his breath as the Farmer swung the other end of the rope from the top of the farmhouse to the roof of the barn. Martha released a confused "Moo" when the rope landed next to her hooves. Parker released a sigh of relief.

"Okay," yelled Molly.

Tyrone placed a ladder against the barn, and then Chet, Carlos, and Tyrone climbed to the roof with all of the farm's pillows (two of which had been on Walter's bed).

Carlos and Chet pressed the pillows against Martha's midsection while Tyrone grabbed the rope and tied it firmly around her. The pillows acted as a buffer between the rope and the cow's hide. Then the boys ran the rope up and over the barn's steel weathervane.

"Moo."

Walter climbed onto the buggy and took the reins.

"Ready?" asked Molly.

Mingo and the Farmer examined the rope threaded through the hook on the chimney, Parker inspected the knot tied to the back of the buggy (he had to admit, it was a better knot than he would have made), and Tyrone, Carlos, and Chet double-checked the rope tied around the cow.

"Ready!" they all responded.

"All right. Slowly," said Molly.

Parker watched as Walter leaned forward from the buggy's bench and gave the horses a gentle rub. "Okay." The horses inched ahead, pulling the buggy and the rope behind it. The rope continued to pull up and over the iron hook on the chimney, down to the cow on the roof, then back across the barn's steel weathervane. Tyrone, Carlos, and Chet held tightly to the other end.

Parker clenched his teeth. Then he felt something brush against his leg. He glanced down to see Outcast worriedly sitting next to him. He leaned over and gave a quick scratch behind the dog's ears.

The rope tugged at Martha, squeezing the pillows against her, but then the horses stopped driving forward.

"Uh-oh," murmured Parker.

"Give it a little more, Walter," called Molly.

Walter gave the reins a flick and the horses took a few steps forward, pulling the buggy and the rope and lurching the cow into the air! Parker gulped. The cow swayed a few feet up and away from the roof—dangling from the rope running between the farmhouse and the barn.

"Whoa," said Parker.

Molly rubbed her temples in amazement. Muttered to herself, "I honestly didn't think this was going to work."

"Nice, Molly," called the Farmer.

"Okay, Walter. Now turn it around carefully. As slowly as you can," said Molly.

Walter pulled the reins and got the horses to gently turn the buggy in the other direction. The cow continued to rise as the horses moved, but when the buggy started going the other way, the cow began to drop, as did the jaws of everyone watching. Molly's pulley system was lowering the cow between the buildings.

Then a pop!

And a crack!

Parker's eyes shot to the farmhouse's roof and grew wide. One of the screws had busted loose and a split was forming down the side of the chimney.

The cow went from being eight feet in the air to seven feet in a split second.

The weathervane creaked.

"This isn't going to hold much longer," called Mingo.

Molly swallowed. "All right, maybe a little faster?"

Walter picked up the pace as the cow continued to be lowered to the ground.

Parker felt his lips tremble. Bit down to get them to stop, but the closer the cow got to the ground the more his lips curled up.

The rope running over the hook began to fray. The hook was ripping the rope as the two rubbed together. And then the rope began to unravel.

Parker gasped.

The weathervane bent.

Outcast barked, which startled the cow. Martha jerked away from the dog, which sent her spinning in a circle on the rope.

Martha spun five feet from the ground. Three feet. The rope continued to unravel. *Snap!* The hook and the remaining screws flew free from the chimney.

Tyrone, Carlos, and Chet were yanked toward the edge of the roof before dropping the rope.

"Look out!" yelled Parker.

The rope and cow plummeted to the earth!

Clomp!

Martha landed on her feet, snorted, and then started eating grass.

Everyone exhaled and clapped for Molly. Parker most of all.

16

PARKER GRABBED TWO fistfuls of soil from a wheelbarrow and sprinkled them over a row of radishes. Then he grabbed two more. And two more after that, and repeated.

The fertilizer smelled awful. Like the ill-advised field trip his class took to a sewage plant in the second grade. Carlos had mentioned something about the smell meaning it was good quality. Parker wished he had anything to cover his nose, or at least didn't have to be so close to it.

"Can't we just use a shovel?" Parker asked.

Chet looked up from his wheelbarrow a few rows over. "Nah, man. Unless you're like a black-belt shoveler? If the radishes get too much soil on top of them they get weighted down and don't grow right. Kind of defeats the purpose of adding more fertilizer in the first place."

Parker nodded, sighed, and kept soiling.

Outcast sat under the fence watching him work. Parker gave the dog a friendly wave before his eyes drifted to the roof of the barn, which was once again cow-free.

He couldn't wrap his head around how Martha got up there. A cow didn't strike him as a climbing creature. Maybe Mingo parked a tractor too close to the barn the night before? The cow could have used it to walk onto the roof. It had to be something like that, right?

As Parker grabbed more soil, he looked across the field at the other boys scattering fertilizer. One by one, each of them turned to the barn's roof and stared for a second or two. Carlos seemed to gaze longer than the others. Clearly they were all wrestling with the same conundrum. Well, everyone except for Chet. Parker hadn't seen Chet look at the roof once.

Parker sprinkled some soil, moved his wheelbarrow forward a few paces, then sprinkled some more. He watched Chet work with his head down. Decided to nudge him. "I still don't understand how she got up there."

Chet kept working. "How who got up where?"

"How—What do you mean who?" Parker shook his head. "How Martha got up on the roof."

Chet continued soiling. "Oh. Are you still thinking about that? She's down now, man, so there's nothing to worry about."

"Nothing to worry about?"

"Yeah, man, nothing to worry about."

Parker stared at his skinny coworker. "You're just going to forget about it?"

Chet shrugged. "Well, we know she didn't jump or take a ramp, and that's all I got. But she's down now, so it doesn't matter anyway."

"What if she gets up there again?"

Chet looked at Parker like that was the craziest thing he had ever heard. "How is a cow going to get on a roof?"

Parker blinked hard. "She did it once already."

"I think we can chalk that up to a fluke."

"A fluke?"

"It means something that wasn't supposed to happen that happened."

"I know what a fluke is, Chet. But I don't understand why you don't care how she got up there."

Chet sighed. "Have you worked on a lot of farms?"

"No."

"Me neither."

Parker waited for more, but nothing came. "What's your point?"

"My point is we aren't exactly experts, man. So we're probably not the ones who should be wasting our time thinking about this. We're not going to solve it, and we have to soil this whole field before we're done for the day."

Parker grabbed two more handfuls of soil and exhaled. Maybe Chet was right.

But Parker couldn't let it go. "I just think—"

He stopped as he heard what sounded like a lawn sprinkler starting behind him, which didn't make sense since the farm had Molly's irrigation system. *Tsk. Tsk. Tsk. Tsk-Tsk-Tsk-Tsk.*

Parker turned.

Less than a yard away, coiled and ready to strike, was a seven-foot rattlesnake.

It took Parker a moment to recognize the reptile. The rattler's scales were the same color as the soil except for the darker diamond shapes that ran down its back. The color drained from Parker's face. His arms went limp, and the fertilizer in his hands trickled through his fingers to the ground.

145

The snake's rattle shook faster and faster.

Parker thought he was going to throw up.

"Don't move, man," said Chet, who stood frozen behind his wheelbarrow.

"Back up slowly," instructed Tyrone as he and the other boys crept toward Parker. Mouths open, breathing heavily.

"Which is it?" whispered Parker. "Stay or move?"

"I'm not exactly sure," admitted Tyrone. Chet shrugged.

The rattlesnake hissed and flicked its tongue, which Parker found more threatening than its tail.

"What do I do?" Parker panted out.

"I'll get help," said Carlos. He took a couple of careful steps from the group before sprinting to the farmhouse.

The snake began to bob and weave. Its head moving forward and backward, a few inches in each direction, threatening to strike.

Parker took one step back.

The rattlesnake shot two feet forward.

Parker felt his heart stop for a couple of beats. He threw his hands in the air.

The snake lifted its head, continued to bob. Hissed again.

"What do I do?" Parker gasped.

The other boys exchanged helpless looks.

Parker held his breath.

The snake hissed. Lunged at Parker, mouth open and fangs out.

Suddenly, Outcast sprang between them with a fierce bark and a snap of his jaws. The rattlesnake changed direction midstrike, turning for the dog.

"No, boy!" yelled Parker.

The dog and snake tangled and tumbled across the field. Dust, dirt, and radishes erupted from the soil.

Outcast growled, bit, and clawed.

The snake hissed and struck the dog, again and again.

"Stop!" screamed Parker.

Chet, Tyrone, and Walter watched in horror as the animals clashed. Spinning left and right, up and down, over rows and rows of radishes.

But after a few seconds the rolling stopped.

What remained of the snake lay still.

Outcast took two proud steps toward Parker, then collapsed on the field.

Parker and the boys ran to the dog. Tears in Parker's eyes, fear across all of their faces.

Parker fell to his knees. Stroked the dog's fur.

"You're going to be okay, boy. Hang in there."

The dog was in bad shape. But he looked at Parker with what energy he had left and smiled.

"You saved me, boy. You saved me!" cried Parker.

Parker picked up the dog and held him to his chest.

The Farmer, Mingo, and Carlos dashed across the field, armed with rakes. They vaulted the fence and hurried to Parker and the boys crouched around Outcast.

"Where's the snake?" called the Farmer.

Tyrone pointed.

"Is everyone okay?" asked Mingo. "Did anyone get bit?"

"My dog," said Parker.

Outcast was barely breathing.

Mingo and Carlos cringed. The Farmer was expressionless.

"Can you take him to the veterinarian?" pleaded Parker.

"Nearest hospital is forty miles," said Mingo. "Vet is probably twice that."

Parker's shoulders slumped. He looked at the Farmer and Mingo. "So what can we do?"

The others just stared. It didn't seem that anyone had an answer, as the little dog struggled to breathe.

Then, without a word, the Farmer bent down and scooped up the dog.

"What are you doing?" Parker asked as he wiped away a tear.

The Farmer ignored Parker and headed back across the field.

Parker turned to Mingo. "Where is he going?"

Molly charged out of the farmhouse, met the Farmer halfway. They had a quick conversation, and then Molly sprinted back into the house, the Farmer walking briskly behind her with the dog.

"What's happening? What is he doing?"

Walter sighed and closed his eyes. "What do you think, Big City? The only thing he can do."

"What can—" Parker's face fell. "You don't mean—He's not gonna—" Parker scrambled to his feet and headed toward the farmhouse. "Wait! Stop! You can't!"

Mingo gently grabbed Parker's arm. "It's okay."

"But he's going to—"

"He's going to do what he can."

Parker opened his mouth to protest, but for one of the few times in his life, he couldn't find the words. So he cried into Mingo's shoulder.

The screen door shut behind the Farmer and the dog.

17

AN HOUR LATER, Parker and his bunkmates sat on top of the picnic table, heads hung, all cried out. The sun was beginning to set. The other boys each had a comforting hand on Parker's back, even Walter.

"Sorry, man," said Chet.

Parker nodded.

Mingo stepped from the barn. Gingerly approached the boys. "Hey, guys, so obviously you should take the rest of the day off. I can patch the field and finish laying the fertilizer by myself. You were almost done anyway."

Parker kept his head down. "I can help you."

"Ah, that's nice of you, bud. But you should take it easy. It won't take me too long."

"It'll be faster if we do it together," said Parker. "And it'll help keep my mind off things."

"I'll help, too," said Chet.

"Us as well," said Tyrone as Carlos gave a confirming nod.

"And me," said Walter.

Mingo offered a small smile of thanks to the boys. "Me too."

Everyone turned to see Molly walking from the farmhouse. She stepped to Parker, offered a hand, and helped him off the table.

One by one, the boys stood and followed Parker, Molly, and Mingo to the abandoned wheelbarrows.

Before digging into the soil, Molly gave Parker's shoulder a squeeze.

—

After the job in the field was finished, Parker felt helpless. He needed to get his thoughts in order and wanted time alone. So, while the others went to rest before dinner, Parker got a ladder from the shed. He propped it against the barn, climbed to the roof, and sat against the bent weathervane. Below him, thousands and thousands of radishes slowly struggled to push themselves through the earth. Each nudging a grain of soil at a time. Their leaves stretching toward the twilight sky. He desperately wanted their strength.

Parker's world seemed different without Outcast—emptier. He wished they'd had a proper goodbye. The dog had saved his life and Parker hadn't even give him a final hug in return. Things had been so chaotic and it happened so fast that he hadn't even thought to. One moment Outcast was there, the next he was carried away.

Parker had never been present for *the end*. The news usually came in a phone call. And in his experience, bad news tended to be delivered to grown-ups first. He remembered his mother getting the call after his grandma Helen passed. And he had a vivid memory of his father's phone ringing before he received the worst news of his life. In both cases, Parker's first feeling wasn't sadness, but pain from not being able to say goodbye.

He stared at the horizon, wondering, hoping, and longing. When he looked down next, he saw the boys leaving the barn. So Parker climbed down, returned the ladder to the shed, and joined them.

There wasn't much talking at dinner. There wasn't much eating, either. The burgers and fries went largely untouched as the boys sat on the fence balancing plates in their laps. They avoided eye contact to prevent another round of tears.

"Maybe we could get another dog," said Carlos.

Tyrone tapped a fry against his plate. "It might bring some happiness back to this place."

"Where would we even get one?" said Walter.

"We could ask Boss," said Chet.

"No," said Parker. "He was a good dog. We shouldn't try to replace him."

The others nodded.

"I should have pulled him off that snake," said Parker.

"No way," said Carlos. "The snake would've bit you, too."

"Without question," said Tyrone.

"And once the dog was bit, it was over, Big City. That was a tough little dog to stay in the fight until the end."

"Tough little dog," confirmed Carlos.

Parker sighed. "Good dog."

"Good dog," repeated Chet.

Parker eyed Outcast's food and water bowls next to the barn. A new wave of sadness washed over him. He set his plate on a post and hopped off the fence. "I should get rid of those."

Parker sniffled as he headed toward the barn.

"I can get them, man," said Chet.

"It's all right," said Parker. He bent to pick up the dishes, then stopped as he heard something echo from the farmhouse.

The others froze, too.

The sound came again. Louder this time. And closer?

Parker stared at the farmhouse.

What was that?

It sounded like...barking?

All eyes went to the back door as it swung open. The Farmer tilted his head and stepped out. He held the door.

The boys heard a "Woof" before exchanging confused expressions.

Then a moment later Outcast happily bounded out of the house and sprinted toward Parker.

Parker's jaw dropped before he beamed. He bent down as the dog leapt into his arms and began furiously licking his face.

"You're okay? I can't believe you're okay!"

Parker hugged the dog. Outcast licked away.

The other boys ran to Parker. Surprise and joy on their faces.

The Farmer stood in the doorway. Molly stepped out next to him and smiled.

Chet stroked the dog's fur.

"How did this happen?" asked Parker.

"I don't know, man. But it feels like magic."

———

Parker tried to thank the Farmer, but the man wouldn't have it. Parker was grateful but overflowing with questions. And the Farmer had no intention of providing answers.

Molly wasn't helpful, either. As she made her way back to the farmhouse, Parker cradled the happy dog in his arms and asked how the Farmer had done it.

"Not all questions have simple answers," she said as she pulled open the screen door.

Parker frowned. "Then can you give me a complicated answer?"

"I just don't think there's anything I can tell you that would be satisfying," she said as she walked inside.

Parker exchanged questioning looks with the dog before calling after Molly, "You're right. That wasn't close to being satisfying."

Back in the barn, Walter let Parker keep his pillow and blanket when the boys went to bed, but Outcast curled up with him anyway. He seemed completely fine. Even in the moonlight Parker could tell that the dog didn't have a single cut or bruise on him. Parker was relieved, thankful, and utterly confused.

"I just don't get it," he whispered to his bunkmates. "It's like nothing happened to him."

"Maybe it wasn't as bad as we thought," replied Carlos.

"Dog was in bad shape, man. We all saw," said Chet.

"What's going on at this farm?" said Parker.

The question hung in the dark.

"I'm serious," said Parker. "What's happening here?"

The boys lay awake wondering, but no one had an answer.

So Parker scratched Outcast behind the ears until the dog fell asleep. And just before he dozed off himself, the dog burped, and Parker smelled the faintest hint of radishes.

18

IT DRIZZLED ON Parker's walk the next morning. Outcast pranced alongside his heels. The gray sky made the farm a deep green.

As the boy and dog passed the farmhouse, Mingo stepped out and motioned with his head for Parker to come over. "Glad you're up. Molly had to work late last night and Boss needs you to deliver an order right away."

"Me?" asked Parker.

"You. It's only a few miles from here." Mingo sighed at the raindrops plopping into a puddle. "I'd go, but this weather is going to make more work. I need to help the guys. It never rains in the summer...."

"Where am I going?"

Mingo pulled a folded piece of paper and a little brown bag from his back pocket. Handed them over. "Directions and the order."

Parker peered into the small bag. Sure enough, there were only two radishes inside. "Wow. So, this is really it?"

"That's the order."

"Huh. And what should I be charging for these?"

"They paid in advance."

Parker looked into the bag again, then looked at Mingo for further explanation.

"You should get going," said Mingo. "This is important."

"Right..."

"Grab a poncho from the shed."

—

The rain fell harder as Parker and Outcast navigated the dirt road. Parker's boots slipped left and right as the ground became mud. The poncho from the supply shed was more of an orange garbage bag with a hood. It kept the rain off, but Parker thought he looked like a traffic cone.

The dog shook water off his fur as they walked, which took Parker's jeans from soggy to soaked.

"Thanks, boy." Parker sighed.

The dog looked up happily.

Parker examined the directions for the eleventh time. Since there weren't street signs, the paper said things like "Take the third left, then the second right," and "Turn down the road with the sycamore tree." It was a step-by-step guide through the muddy cornfield maze to "The Tim O'Malley Farm," all written in beautiful penmanship. He wondered if it was Molly's handwriting.

Unfortunately, the more he looked at the directions, the wetter the paper became. And the wetter the paper became, the more the ink ran. Before long, the final two steps were unreadable. What was it that they said? The second-to-last one seemed to say "Veer left," but he couldn't make out where. And the last line looked like it said something about...Did that say "platypus"?

Parker was hopelessly lost.

And drenched.

He squinted at the directions. Willed the words to unsmear with his mind. But they became blurrier in the rain, so he tucked them away under the poncho, figuring he'd need whatever was still readable to get back.

Thunder rumbled.

"Great..."

He looked at the dog. Shrugged. "I don't really know what we're supposed to do."

Outcast shook himself off all over Parker again. Took a seat.

"Not what I would've suggested."

Parker watched as his muddy footprints washed away in the rain. He looked forward and back. "Do you think we passed it?"

The dog smiled.

Parker began jumping to try to see over the tops of the cornfields. He couldn't. And with each jump, it became harder to get off the ground, as the slippery mud became sticky.

"Where should we go?"

Outcast didn't seem to know.

So Parker sat next to the dog and wished they could get out of the rain.

And wished all of these houses in town weren't so many miles apart.

And wished he had taken better care of the directions.

They had missed breakfast. The other boys were probably eating lunch by now.

He looked at the fields around them. Wondered if they could eat corn raw. It was probably safe, but he didn't want to risk it.

So he waited.

And waited.

And waited until he heard another rumble. Quieter this time, but the sound seemed endless. It became louder. Like the storm was growing.

But it wasn't thunder.

He saw the headlights first—a white pickup truck making its way through mud and rain.

Parker's hands shot up to wave it down.

The truck slowed. Dirt was splattered across its fenders. The window rolled down, revealing an older couple clad in denim in the cab.

"Thanks for stopping," said Parker.

"You strike me as someone who should get out of the rain," said the old man behind the wheel.

"Just walking my dog on this gorgeous day," said Parker. Thunder cracked again.

The old man smiled. Parker's eyes went wide as he got a better look at the man's bushy gray mustache.

"Where you headed, son?"

Parker glared at the mustache. Stole a glance at the sky.

"Son?"

"Um. Any chance you know where the O'Malley Farm is?"

The couple chuckled. "It's right up the road. Hop in the back," said the old woman.

"Are you sure?"

The couple grinned. "You could hit it with a rock from here. Hop in!"

Parker looked uneasily at Outcast, picked up the dog, and hurried to the truck bed. As he pulled down the gate and put Outcast in, he noticed a younger boy already sitting there under a red umbrella. The boy was using a rope as a makeshift seat belt.

"Hi," said Parker.

"Hi," said the younger boy.

Parker climbed up, closed the gate, and used another piece of rope tied to the truck's bed to secure himself. The boy tilted his umbrella to share. Parker nodded his thanks.

The truck lurched forward and bounced along its way.

The younger kid stuck out a hand. "Milo."

Parker shook it. "Parker. Did you come with the truck when these people bought it?"

The kid laughed. "They're my grandparents. I like your garbage bag."

"Thanks. It's reversible. And I think also recycled."

"Where are you going? It's so wet out."

"Is it?" Parker leaned away from the umbrella and gazed up at rain pouring down. The water pounded his face and made the boy smile. "I'm going to the O'Malley Farm."

"You Mr. O'Malley's nephew or something?"

"Making a delivery. Got a little lost."

The road split and the truck veered to the left, the dog cheerily sliding across the vehicle's floor as they turned.

"First day on the job?"

"Pretty much."

The truck came to a stop in front of a little pink farmhouse. "This is it," said Milo.

"That was fast."

"You were close," the younger boy said with a shrug.

The boys shook hands again before Parker and Outcast climbed out.

"You should probably know where you're going the next time you head into a storm like this," said the old man through the window.

"I'll consider it," said Parker. "Thanks for the lift."

The old couple nodded.

Parker waved as Milo and his grandparents drove off. He watched the truck until it disappeared. Then the rain stopped.

As he made his way to the little pink house, he smirked at the wooden platypus carving on top of the mailbox.

Before Parker could knock, the front door flew open.

A man in his thirties stood on the other side of the doorway. It didn't look like he had showered or shaved in days. There was a tear in his eye. "You came," the man said with relief. "I didn't think you were coming."

Parker frowned at the man. Rainwater dripped off his poncho onto the front porch. "I'm Parker...."

"But from the farm, yes?"

"Yeah. You're Tim O'Malley?"

"My father. They're for him." The man ran a nervous hand through his hair. "You brought them?"

Parker reached into his back pocket uneasily. Pulled out the brown paper bag. The man's face lit up as Parker handed over the radishes.

"Thank you! Oh, thank you, thank you, thank you! You don't know what this means to us." The man turned and called to someone in the house, "I have them! They're here!" Then the man closed the door in Parker's face.

Parker heard footsteps as the man ran to another room. He stared at the door, trying to figure out what just happened.

It didn't look like Outcast knew, either.

Obviously Parker was going to have to try one of the farm's radishes.

19

PARKER IMPRESSED HIMSELF by only tak-
ing two wrong turns on the journey back. He nearly
made a third, but before he did, he spotted the top of
the farm's green water tower and course-corrected. The
sun had come out, and the sky was nothing but blue.

When he got to the farm he returned the poncho to
the shed, grabbed a leftover sandwich from the picnic
table, and spotted Mingo, Molly, and the boys using
garden hoes and rakes in the field.

Parker ripped off part of the sandwich for the dog,
then devoured the rest himself as they moseyed toward
the others.

The neat rows that the crops grew in weren't so neat anymore. Some of the edges had crumbled or begun to lean in a less-than-straight manner.

Mingo looked up with sweat on his brow. "Any problems?"

"I got a little lost, but I made it."

"Great, bud. We're way behind." Mingo leaned his garden hoe against the blue fence. "Why don't you take over here?" Mingo hurried off toward the supply shed.

Parker eyed the garden hoe. Tried to remember if he'd ever seen one in person. Watched the other boys working, then analyzed the hoe again.

"It helps if you pick it up."

Parker glanced over as Molly stepped to the fence, a hoe propped against her shoulder.

"I was easing into it," he said. "Worried I might get a cramp if I start so soon after eating."

"Just watch me for a second," Molly said as she turned and planted her feet.

Parker grabbed the tool and came in close as Molly drove her garden hoe into the soil. Outcast took a seat under the fence.

Parker watched as Molly dragged the hoe along the edge of a row of radishes, reshaping the border that had washed away in the heavy rain. She lifted and dropped the hoe again, carving, pushing, and pulling the soil, until the damaged row became a straight line again.

"It's a simple concept," Molly explained as she worked the garden hoe back and forth. "Farmers have essentially been doing the same thing for thousands of years. It just takes a little muscle and focus. We want to keep the good topsoil hugging the crop. The topsoil has the most nutrients, so we want to work it so it stays in place and holds the water that we give the radishes. Rain kind of has its own plan for things. Raindrops from a storm don't really all fall in the same direction, so everything gets knocked this way and that, and we want the plants to be able to absorb as many nutrients as they can. That's why we shape the fields into these rows. Make sense?"

"Makes sense," said Parker.

"Good. Get in there."

Parker stepped into Molly's place and began working the soil. Molly watched him. "You're a natural."

"Come on. I'm trying."

"I'm serious. You're getting it."

Parker shrugged and felt his face become warm.

"Parker, are you blushing?"

"No."

"You're blushing."

He grinned. "Leave me alone."

"Hey, look who's a natural," said Mingo as he climbed the fence with a bucket.

Molly laughed. "See? Told you."

Parker shook his head as he carved the earth. "How long have you been doing this, Mingo?"

"You mean been on this farm?"

"Yeah."

Mingo crouched, picked up a pebble, and tossed it into his bucket. "Since I was a little older than you. But when you find where you want to be and what you want to be doing, sometimes if you're lucky you get to keep doing it."

"I like that," said Parker.

"So do I, bud." Mingo took his bucket and moved down the pen, on the hunt for stray pebbles. Molly nodded at Parker before following Mingo with her garden hoe.

Parker watched them cross the field. Wondered how much they knew about this place. They had to agree there was something strange about the deliveries and emergency radish orders in the middle of the night, right? And what had happened to the cow and the dog? Those weren't things that someone could dismiss and ignore. Well, maybe Chet could.

Parker returned his attention to the rows in front of him, throwing his mind and body into the work. He kept his head down, but before long found himself focusing on the radishes rather than the rows. He glanced at the others, all busy with their own work. Then looked back at the radish tops. And when he was sure no one was looking, he crouched, pulled a radish from the ground, and slipped it into his pocket.

"Big City."

Parker froze. Waited for his heart to beat again before peeking up to see Walter staring down at him.

"Where'd you go this morning?" asked Walter.

Parker gulped. Got to his feet. "Delivery for Boss," he said as naturally as he could.

"Really? Hey, Tyrone?"

"Yes?" Tyrone called from across the field.

"Big City ran a delivery for Boss."

Parker let out a sigh of relief. Walter must not have seen him take the radish.

"That's unexpected," said Tyrone.

"Yeah," said Carlos from farther ahead. "I thought only Mingo and Molly made deliveries. Hey, Mingo?"

"Yeah?" said Mingo from the far end of the pen.

"How come Parker got to go on a delivery?" asked Carlos.

"Boss asked for him specifically," said Mingo. "I guess he noticed the effort he's put in lately."

"He sees everything from up there," said Molly.

Parker glanced at the top floor of the farmhouse. And he felt the radish in his pocket press against his thigh as he worked.

Parker waited in bed until he was sure everyone else was asleep. Even the dog. Then he waited longer.

The moonlight through the window was unusually bright after the storm.

Parker reached into his pajama pocket and took out the radish. Brushed it off on the side of his cot. He looked around the room, drew in a deep breath, and took a bite.

Crunch.

He didn't think it was awful, but it certainly wasn't incredible. It tasted like, well, a radish.

He shrugged and took another bite. And since radishes aren't that big, that was it. He was left with a few radish leaves, and questions as to what the big deal was.

He finished chewing and swallowed. Hid the leaves under his mattress to dispose of later.

Parker was underwhelmed, but, hey, he figured some people must really like radishes.

He lay down and felt guilty. Reached beneath the cot and pulled the photograph of his mother from the pocket in his suitcase. Smiled at the picture. Wondered if she would have tried a radish. Probably not. She was fun, but always a rule-follower. She'd probably be disappointed if she knew. The thought made Parker feel worse.

And then something strange happened: His head felt light. No. Wait. It wasn't just his head, it was his whole body.

He studied his hands as they began to tingle. Then looked down at his legs. And that was when he noticed he wasn't on the bed anymore.

He was floating two feet up and rising.

Parker's eyes bulged. He dropped the frame on the mattress and reached for the cot, but the movement only shook the itchy blanket off him and onto the floor. He continued to rise as panic set in. He would yell, but he was too scared. Plus, he had a hunch that the others wouldn't take his aversion to gravity that well.

Bonk. He hit his head on the ceiling. He cringed but did his best not to make a sound. He rubbed his skull. The pain washed away the initial shock.

He looked at the floor fifteen feet below—the others asleep. He thought it was odd seeing the room

from this angle. Then he wondered how he would get down.

Maybe he could propel himself? He pushed off the ceiling, glided a few feet toward his bed, then floated back up. *Bonk.*

Parker rubbed his head and worried that he might be stuck.

His eyes went to the wooden slats that covered the ceiling. The creases where the boards connected seemed big enough to work as fingerholds. So he stuck his fingers in and began pulling himself across the ceiling one slat at time until he reached a support beam. Carefully, he pulled himself down the rafter. When he made it to the bottom of the beam, he looked for a place to go next.

The front door was five feet below. Maybe he could thrust himself down to the top of its frame? It was worth a shot. Especially without options.

Parker shimmied around and planted his feet on the underside of the beam. He hung upside down, but it felt like gravity was pushing him *up*. He took a deep breath, then kicked off as hard as he could. He glided, strained to reach.

His body slowed.

Ten inches from the doorframe.

Six inches.

He was barely moving.

Three inches.

He stretched until he hurt.

One inch.

He wasn't going to make it. He willed himself to stretch another quarter of an inch.

Contact! His fingertips brushed against the doorframe and he held.

But now what?

He looked around the room. Maybe if he flung himself to the doorknob he could swing from bed to bed until he made it back to his own? Parker peered down. Launched his body to the doorknob and grabbed it. Easy! He was getting good at this.

Then the knob turned, and the door opened into the night. Parker went along for the ride, slamming his heels against the frame along the way.

He winced and accidentally let go. Then gasped as he floated away. Above the barn, above the farm, above the world, up toward the starry sky.

Parker began to regret eating the radish.

And he was reasonably certain his dream about the flying goat hadn't been a dream at all. Carlos probably hadn't been daydreaming, either. Parker also had a pretty good idea how Martha ended up on the roof after wandering from the corral.

He continued to rise. The farmhouse grew tinier, and the clouds grew closer. But the look of sheer terror on his face morphed into a smile. He realized he wasn't going to sail off into space. If a cow could come down, then so could he. Better still, the goat had managed to glide along a few feet off the ground. Maybe he could control where he was going.

Parker tried to will himself left, then right with his mind. It didn't work. He just went up.

Maybe he could walk through the sky? He took a

few air steps—his feet spun like they were pedaling an invisible bicycle, and he did a somersault. Progress, but not what he was looking for.

Perhaps if he "swam"?

He thought back to his junior lifeguard training course at the Leisure Centre. Maybe the breaststroke? He gave it a shot. Like a frog swimming through the air, he was thrilled to find that it worked. His body moved in the direction he swam. Up, down, and to either side. The wind gently blew his hair. And the ground sat a mile below.

Parker Kelbrook was flying.

And he was ecstatic.

He flipped onto his back to get a better view of the twinkling stars. Then spun into a barrel roll and became delightfully dizzy. Parker twisted this way and that, soared up, and sped down like he was gliding on his own private roller coaster. And then he startled himself with a scream of joy.

Parker flew across the sky, faster and faster, down and up, into clouds and out again.

And before he knew it, he couldn't see the barn. Or at least he wasn't sure if he could see his barn. He could see dozens of farms, but from that high up they all looked the same. A massive grid of interchangeable squares and rectangles below.

"Huh," he mumbled as he realized he'd lost his sense of direction while spinning. He didn't have a clue which part of the grid he'd come from.

Then without warning, Parker plummeted fifty feet. He clenched his eyes shut and he yelped. He wasn't sure if either of those things helped, but he stabilized after he did.

Then he plunged seventy-five more feet and knew he was in trouble. He yelled again and evened out for a split second before he fell twisting toward the ground.

Acres of cornfields rushed at him as he fell, the wind vibrating and pushing back his face. The man with the mustache flashed in his mind. Parker was a skydiver without a parachute.

His yelling did nothing to slow the fall. And luckily (or unluckily) he was so high up that no one could hear him.

The fields got closer and closer.

Parker swam toward the stars with all his might, harder and harder, until he curved just enough to slow his descent and barely pull up. And as he did, he skimmed the top of a cornfield, with ears of corn and leaves knocking his head and shoulders until he came to a stop and found himself cradled in the field.

Then the cornstalks that held him buckled and he fell the final two feet to the ground.

Parker caught his breath and tried to understand what just happened.

He had flown.

And landed. He wasn't great at that part.

20

PARKER WAS OKAY other than a few scrapes and bruises, but for the second time in twenty-four hours he was lost. He had spun so much and flown so long that he didn't know whether he was blocks or miles from the barn. Figuring there was little chance of being rescued by another white pickup, he brushed off his pajamas, flipped an imaginary coin, and headed left under the moonlight.

He spent more time gazing at the stars than looking forward as he stumbled through countless fields. He couldn't wait to get back into the clouds. Eventually he found himself staggering past the train station. He thought of his first walk with Molly. He could recall every step. So he retraced those steps, and before he knew it, he was hobbling down the road toward the farm as the first hints of sunlight crept over the horizon.

As Parker wondered whether he would run into Molly on her morning walk, a window opened on the top floor of the farmhouse and she stuck out her head. Sometimes the world is funny like that.

Molly frowned. "Why are you outside in your pajamas?"

"The lady who sold them to me said they were appropriate for all occasions."

"Is that a leaf in your hair?"

Parker ran his hands over his scalp and pulled out a leaf from an ear of corn. He smiled up at Molly. "I heard it works as a natural conditioner. Are you coming down? I can put a bunch on your head."

"Some other time. Have to pack. We're leaving right after the harvest."

"Harvest?"

～

Parker stood in a pen with Carlos and Tyrone after breakfast. Each boy had an empty wicker basket by his feet, and held a hand fork—a three-pronged tool used for gardening, the prongs as long as fingers. The dog slept under the fence.

Mingo, Walter, and Chet were crouched by their own baskets in the next pen, while the Farmer and Molly worked the next pen over from that.

Two refrigerator trucks had been parked beside the farmhouse.

"They grow faster than you'd think," Tyrone explained to Parker. "It's rather extraordinary."

"They're ready to harvest four weeks after we plant them," said Carlos.

"We're picking the first three pens today, and then we'll reseed tomorrow," said Tyrone. "Then we harvest the fourth pen in two weeks."

"They're staggered that way so Boss always has at least some radishes available," said Carlos.

Parker asked the question that hadn't left his mind since he floated up from his cot, "Available for what? Where are they going?"

"Boss and Molly take their truck east, then west," said Carlos.

"While Mingo journeys north, then south," said Tyrone.

"But to who specifically?" asked Parker.

Tyrone shrugged. "I suppose distributors and benefactors."

"Benefactors?" Parker wondered who these mysterious

people were that bought magical radishes. From experience, he couldn't blame them for wanting to fly.

"Folks who finance what we do here. Who keep the heartland going," said Tyrone.

"Boss and Molly send radishes all over the country," said Carlos.

"We're thinking more along the lines of lettuce for our own farm."

"Or artichokes."

Tyrone grimaced. "Why do you keep bringing up artichokes, Carlos? You know how temperamental they are with weather."

"But we love artichokes."

"And they attract so many pests."

"Because they're delicious."

Tyrone patted Carlos on the back. "We'll get there eventually, but baby steps, my friend. Baby steps."

Carlos nodded and shook Tyrone's hand.

Parker blinked and turned to the field. "So what do we do?"

Tyrone squatted next to his basket and demonstrated. "You insert the hand fork into the soil about two inches from the radish at an angle so you can get underneath it with the prongs and carefully push the plant up by the root. Then you pull from the leaves so the radish comes free from the soil." Three perfect radishes rose from the earth on the hand fork. "Then just give them a gentle shake to get rid of excess dirt, before dropping them in the basket."

"And when the basket gets full, you load it into the truck and grab another basket," said Carlos.

Parker stared into his empty basket.

"Easy enough?" asked Carlos.

"Easy enough," said Parker.

"Splendid," said Tyrone. "Now let's all do that about a thousand times."

Parker sighed and the boys got to work. He lifted a few forkfuls of radishes from the ground and into his basket, then paused as something occurred to him. "If Boss and Mingo are driving out of town, who's watching us while they're gone?"

"Mingo isn't traveling as far. He'll return late this evening," said Tyrone. "But trust me, Parker, you thought pulling weeds was challenging? This is grueling. A radish isn't exactly the heaviest thing in the world, but perform a thousand repetitions of anything and you'll feel it. Especially after hauling full baskets across the farm all day. We're going to want to go straight to bed when we finish."

"Got it," said Parker. But he knew no matter how much more exhausted he became he was going to sneak away to eat another radish that evening.

He couldn't wait.

⁓

Parker dozed off while filling his seventh basket, which caused his left arm to slip and poke the hand fork into his knee. He was wide-awake after that. He groaned, then filled two more baskets. Every so often his head tilted toward the clouds and a smile snuck across his face.

He was surprised to discover that Carlos and Tyrone were right about every radish being different. Some had slight variations in colors. Some were long. Others short. Most round. Some pencil-thin. Many had twists and curves. Nearly all had wrinkles and distinguishing spots. They certainly weren't the most attractive things Parker had ever seen.

Parker's ninth basket was the last one placed in the first refrigerator truck. Mingo said a quick goodbye and drove north. Outcast barked as he left.

When Parker, Tyrone, and Carlos finished harvesting their pen, they joined Walter and Chet in the next pen over. When the boys finished that one, they joined Molly and the Farmer and helped pull those radishes as well.

Then the Farmer and Molly drove east. They left dinner for the boys, but as Tyrone promised, Parker wanted to go straight to bed. His body felt like jelly. He figured he could take a nap before slipping away that evening.

He struggled to put one foot in front of the other as he and the boys made their way to the barn. Outcast proudly strutted alongside him. Parker felt an arm slip around his shoulder and was startled to discover that it was Walter's.

"So, what did it taste like, Big City?"

"What did wha—" Parker's words trickled off, and a knot formed in his stomach. He tried to pull away from the bigger boy, but Walter held on.

"Come on, Big City, we've all wondered."

"Wondered what?" Tyrone asked as he came up behind them.

"Nothing," said Parker.

"Ah, I don't think it's nothing," said Walter. "Big City here pocketed a radish yesterday."

185

Chet looked back from up ahead and sighed. "I told you we weren't supposed to do that, man. Boss only has a few rules."

"Oh, I think Big City knew he wasn't supposed to take it. You should have seen him. He thought he was being really slick."

Parker hung his head.

"So what was it like?" asked Tyrone. "I've never been a huge proponent of radishes, but I figure these must be pretty good."

"Yeah, I've always kind of wondered, too," said Carlos.

"Oh. Well, uh. It was no big deal really," said Parker.

"Come on."

"Well, it, um," said Parker. "It, um, kind of just tasted like a radish."

"That's it?" asked Carlos.

"Well. Yeah."

"I don't know, Big City," Walter said with a smile, "it feels like there's something you're not telling us."

21

THE SUN SET as Parker and the boys stood in a corner of the unpicked pen contemplating the two dozen rows of radishes. Outcast panted at Parker's heels.

"This is dumb, man. We shouldn't do this," said Chet.

"It's only five radishes," said Walter. "Boss isn't going to miss them. What are you waiting for, Big City? Pick them for us."

"Me?"

"Yeah," said Walter. "You."

Picking five radishes felt astronomically worse than picking one. But the veins throbbing in Walter's neck and biceps were motivating.

Chet fidgeted with his shirtsleeves and bit his lip.

"This is wrong," he mumbled before climbing the fence and heading to the barn.

The other boys watched him go.

"All right, four," said Walter.

Parker looked at Carlos and Tyrone. "You guys sure you want to do this?"

"Honestly, it feels critical to our vocational education," said Tyrone.

"Yeah, almost like it would be stupid for us to not try one," said Carlos. "Plus, it's just one radish, right?"

"Do it, Big City."

Parker glanced at the barn.

"Do it."

Parker exhaled, crouched, and inspected the radishes at his feet. They were smaller than the ones they had picked from the other pens that morning, since they were two weeks behind in growth. He was surprised he'd never noticed that. He sighed and gently pulled four of the biggest radishes he could find. He handed one to each of the boys. They studied them like they hadn't seen radishes before, each waiting for another to take the first bite.

"On three?" suggested Parker.

"You first," said Walter.

Parker nodded, then bit the radish away from its leaves in a single bite. *Crunch.*

The other boys shrugged and followed suit.

Outcast whimpered.

And they waited.

"How long does it take?" asked Carlos.

Before Parker could answer, Tyrone drifted off the ground.

"Whoa!"

Tyrone was three feet up when Carlos rose with a chuckle. Parker and Walter left the ground in quick succession. The boys were all smiles.

The dog stared blankly before running to the barn. "It's okay, boy," called Parker. But the dog wasn't having it. As soon as he reached the door, he began scratching for Chet to let him in.

The boys exchanged smiles as they continued to rise while trying to master flight. Walter couldn't stop giggling as his air-bicycle pedaling sent him somersaulting up. Carlos did his best superhero pose in an attempt to shoot across the sky, but he simply floated higher.

"How do we do it, Parker?" asked Tyrone. "Is it possible to steer?"

"Try swimming," said Parker. "Watch." He demonstrated with a frog kick, propelling himself over the field.

"Ah," said Carlos, and flipped into a backstroke.

Walter dog-paddled while Tyrone executed perfect butterfly strokes.

The boys were fearless, zipping up and down and across the farm. And this time, Parker kept the farmhouse in sight as he explored.

"This is incredible!" shouted Tyrone.

The boys circled the water tower, then swooped down to the corral, skimming inches above the animals' heads. "Baa," said the goats.

Then the boys shot straight up. Climbing higher and higher and higher, laughing and spinning along the way. The boys nose-dived, and swerved, and howled. Life in the air was spectacular.

"I can't believe you were going to keep this to yourself," called Tyrone.

"No wonder Boss didn't want us to eat any of these," said Walter. "We'd never get any work done!"

"The only problem is landing," called Parker as he darted through a cloud.

"Huh?"

"Landing," repeated Parker. "I don't know how to land."

"Seriously?" said Tyrone.

"Yeah," said Parker. "Honestly, it feels like something I should have brought up earlier." As soon as he got the words out, Walter plummeted fifty feet and screamed. Mouths dropped open and eyes went wide.

Parker knew they needed to get down as quickly as possible, but the ground seemed hopelessly far below. His heart raced as he searched for an elevated place to land. "The roof of the farmhouse! Hurry!"

Carlos dropped thirty feet before regaining control. Parker fell seventy. And Tyrone fell fifteen. The boys followed Parker as he raced to the farmhouse. "Just get as low as you can," he called.

Tyrone yelped as he fell another thirty-five feet. "I don't think that'll be a problem!"

Parker flailed his arms and legs backward to slow down as he rocketed toward the roof. The others did the same. Walter ran out of gas first. He dropped the final seven feet onto the farmhouse and landed on his shoulder with an "Oof." Then gravity took over and he rolled down the shingles.

"Hang on!" yelled Carlos.

Walter tried to grab onto anything to stop his roll before he shot from the end of the roof. He was unsuccessful and flew off the side of the farmhouse. Miraculously, he caught the rain gutter just before slamming into the side of the building. But he hung on, three stories up.

The others didn't fare much better. One by one they thumped onto the roof, rolled down the shingles, grabbed the rain gutter at the last possible moment, and crashed into the side of the house.

They dangled, panting, grateful to be alive.

"Wow," said Tyrone.

"Uh-huh," said Parker.

"I think I solved the mystery of the falling man," said Carlos. "Feels like some of you owe me an apology."

"I still say you dreamed that," said Walter.

Carlos shook his head. "Ah, come on."

Tyrone smiled at the sky. "We must do that again."

"Yep," said Parker.

———

The boys climbed onto the roof, jimmied a window, and stepped inside the farmhouse's office.

A simple chair sat behind a pair of phones on a wooden dining room table being used as a desk, but those were the least interesting things in the office. The rest of the room was covered with thirty stacks of newspapers, each stack five feet high. The boys could barely move.

"Whoa," said Parker. "They're hoarders."

"This has to be every newspaper Boss ever received," said Walter.

"This one's from today," announced Parker as he pulled the *Reno Gazette* from the top of a stack. "And from Nevada."

Carlos busied himself with another pile across the room. "Illinois. Indiana. Ohio. All from today, too."

"You're joking," said Parker.

"Here as well," Tyrone said as he shuffled through another stack. "They're all different. All the papers in this stack are from California."

"Florida and Georgia over here," said Carlos.

"These are Connecticut," said Walter. "And Maine. New York. Today, today, today."

Parker looked around uneasily. "This is weird. And not just the papers. Being in this house feels like we're reading someone's diary. Do you know what I mean? We should get out of here."

The other boys nodded, seemingly on the same page. Walter led the way out of the office and down two flights of stairs.

The rest of the farmhouse was covered in hardwood and red wallpaper with zebras and hippopotamuses painted on it. Small brass chandeliers hung on each floor. The house was spotless and felt older than Parker would have guessed.

As the boys followed Walter out the front door,

something caught Parker's attention in the foyer. Sitting on an end table was a photograph of the Farmer holding a baby. He wondered if it was Molly. The Farmer appeared to be a decade or so younger and he looked happy, which made Parker stop. He'd never seen the Farmer smile.

Parker slipped out of the house and carefully closed the front door behind him. Outside, the other boys were already plotting.

"So, obviously we need a better way to land," said Walter.

Four sets of eyes scanned the farm.

Tyrone thrust a finger into the air. "A haystack!"

Parker's nose wrinkled. "Where do we have a haystack?"

"We'll make one," explained Carlos.

"This way," said Walter as they jogged to the corral.

Walter unhooked the old bungee cord that kept the gate closed, ran past the cows and goats, and grabbed a bale of hay from one of the massive stacks. The other boys did the same, then ran the bales into the field, and repeated until sixteen bricks of hay sat outside the first pen.

"Now what?" asked Parker. "These don't seem any softer than the ground."

"Now we open them," said Walter as he pulled a rusty pocketknife from his jeans and cut the twine hugging the first bale.

Parker crossed his arms. "Are you guys sure about this?"

Carlos began ripping Walter's bale apart and tossing it into a pile. "We'll just put the hay next to the corral when we finish."

"Won't Mingo notice?"

"He won't mind," said Tyrone as he helped Walter with another bale. "As long as the animals eat, he's content. He has to open these eventually anyway. Ultimately, we're making his life easier."

Parker shrugged and helped make the stack.

Forty minutes later the moon was shining and the boys were back in the pen with the radishes.

Two minutes after that they were in the air, shrieking and cheering, as the animals strolled out of the corral. The bungee cord that kept the gate shut hadn't been properly latched.

—

It didn't take long for the animals to end up in the radishes.

The horses floated only a few inches above the field.

At first it seemed they were afraid of heights, but on closer inspection it became clear that they were obsessed with eating radishes. They gobbled them by the mouthful, row after row, like they hadn't eaten in weeks (though Mingo had fed them an hour before he left). Meanwhile, the goats flew death-defying loops over the farmhouse.

Plummeting through the air before landing was scary for Parker, but not as scary as soaring toward a seventeen-hundred-pound flying cow. And arguably less expected.

"Cow!" shouted Carlos.

"What the—" Parker made a split-second decision to fly over Martha as she sailed out of nowhere. Tyrone was flying right behind him and decided to go under. Luckily the cow flew straight. Once again, an animal's laziness was an asset to those on the farm. Unfortunately, Martha continued flying straight until she rammed the water tower at four and a half miles per hour.

Boom.

"Moo."

As the cow gracefully landed on the grass, the holding tank on top of the tower teetered. Parker held his breath as the whites of his eyes grew.

The massive tank tipped from the tower and smashed onto the field.

The few radishes left uneaten by the boys and the animals were squashed by the debris as a flood of water erupted from the tank.

Chet bolted from the barn, startled by the commotion as Parker and the others landed in the haystack. The boys gaped slack-jawed at the mess.

Even in the moonlight it was clear the crop was no more.

22

CHET SURVEYED THE damage before frowning at Parker. "You guys did a bad thing, man."

"I know."

Tyrone, Carlos, and Walter cringed at the mess.

Chet nodded. "We should get to work." He hopped the fence to the shed to gather shovels, buckets, and rakes, pitching in without complaining.

Little was said over the next few hours. The boys cleaned what they could.

The maple tree next to the farmhouse was climbed, and the goat that was stuck in its branches was carried down. And the goat that had gotten itself jammed in the tire swing was gently removed.

The hay was placed next to the corral, and the animals were led inside, then the gate was firmly latched.

The water tank was deemed beyond repair, so the boys began to haul its remains to the side of the barn. And that was what the boys were guiltily doing when Mingo climbed out of his refrigerator truck and shuffled over.

As Mingo processed the swamped, pummeled disaster of a field, Parker worried he was going to be sick. The other boys' eyes went wide and their shoulders slumped. Parker braced himself for Mingo to erupt. Scanned the ground for a piece of the wreckage to hide behind. "Mingo, we—"

But Mingo stayed calm. He shook his head. "Let's go to bed, guys. We can address this with fresh eyes and rested muscles tomorrow."

"It was an accident," explained Parker.

"And yet it happened all the same, bud."

The cleanup resumed the next morning with Outcast watching and providing moral support.

By midmorning, the debris from the tank had been cleared.

By lunch, no noticeable progress had been made in

creating new rows for radishes to be planted in the fourth pen. No matter how the soil was carved, it caved into itself as soon as the garden hoes were pulled away. "It's just too wet, fellas," explained Mingo. "We're going to have to wait another day or so for the sun to dry out the soil."

So they began the tedious process of reseeding the first three pens. The boys were given buckets full of dark brown, oval-shaped seeds. Every seed half the size of a popcorn kernel. Then they used their garden hoes to dig trenches about an inch deep in each of the pens' rows, before dropping seeds about a knuckle's length apart along each trench and then covering the seeds with topsoil. It took hours to seed the field, and hours more to water the seeds after they were planted. But by dinner, the Farmer and Molly returned to find the boys watching mud dry in the fourth pen, and not a single radish growing on the entire farm.

The Farmer gazed at the soggy, barren enclosure. The giant of a man appeared small. Parker worried a gust of wind might carry the

Farmer away. He seemed absolutely devastated. And Parker had never felt worse.

"Sorry, Boss," said Carlos.

"We're doing everything we can to fix it," said Parker.

"My aunt can reimburse you for the money you lost from the harvest and the cost of a new water tank," said Walter.

"We didn't intend for this to happen," said Tyrone.

The Farmer sighed. A mask fell over his face as he headed toward the house. It was like ice water pumped through his veins.

Molly, on the other hand, looked like her skin was boiling, but she left without saying anything to the boys, either.

"Molly. Wait," called Parker.

She didn't look back.

———

The Farmer stayed out of sight for the next few days. No matter what Parker and the boys did, he wouldn't leave the house.

They tried knocking.

They slid letters of apology under the front door.

They walked all the way to town to bring back a delicious gourmet meal.

And after some begging, pleading, and apologizing, Walter was able to convince his aunt to ship a new water tank for the tower.

But mostly, Parker and the boys worked as hard as possible.

And Parker rose early each morning to try to talk to Molly. He would wait and hope that she'd leave the farmhouse to run an errand or go on a walk. Whenever they saw each other, she said, "Don't talk to me," and he said, "I'm sorry."

Then Parker and the guys would spend the morning pulling weeds. When they finished, they would clean anything and everything. If it were possible for a farm to sparkle, this one would have. When the boys ran out of things to clean, maintain, and repair, they stood outside with garden hoes until the moon rose, attempting to will the mud in the fourth pen to dry.

Occasionally Parker caught Molly peering down from her third-story window. She turned away whenever he tried to wave.

But the Farmer remained absent.

Three days after the incident Tyrone stood up from the field and announced that the soil had dried enough to hold. The boys grabbed their tools and went to work. Parker discovered that creating new rows was more challenging than mending existing ones. The soil had to be forced into shape, pounded again and again.

There was little talking that afternoon and no noise other than the scraping and thumping of dirt. Somehow even the animals knew to be quiet and the wind knew not to blow. So when the phone rang in the farmhouse, all of the boys heard. Fifteen minutes later, the back door of the house opened and the Farmer tilted his head to step out.

The boys held their breaths as the Farmer strode across the field and up to Parker. "Come with me."

Parker swallowed and set his garden hoe against the fence.

The boy guiltily followed the Farmer like an inmate trailing an executioner as they rounded the far side of the house. When they reached the garage, the Farmer lifted the giant door to reveal a classic red truck.

Parker had only seen pickups like it in pictures and old movies. It looked like it was from the 1940s, but he wasn't convinced it had ever been driven. It was the most beautiful vehicle he had ever seen.

"Wow." Parker got a closer look. Smiled through the glass at the leather interior.

"Get in," said the Farmer.

Parker's heart sank. "Look, I know I said I wanted

to go home, but that was a while ago. I want to make things right. And I'd like to stay a part of this if you'll let me. I mean, I know whatever is happening on this farm is special, even though I'm still not sure what we're doing here in the grand scheme of things."

"You'll see," said the Farmer.

"I'll see?"

"You'll see."

Parker tilted his head and tried to get a read on the man. "I'll see what?"

"Get in the truck."

"Do I need my luggage?"

"Get in the truck, Parker. I'm going to show you what we do here."

"Oh." Parker wasn't expecting that. He opened the passenger door and hopped in. "That's great. Actually, I have quite a few questions. So, what exactly—"

"Please stop talking."

"Okay."

The Farmer climbed in, started the truck, and drove off the property.

23

PARKER AND THE Farmer rode in silence as walls of corn sped by. The boy twiddled his thumbs. The man watched the dirt road. The sun descended.

"Should we listen to the radio?" Parker asked.

The Farmer kept driving.

Parker sighed. "Probably not much of a signal out here."

After a while Parker became nervous. Where were they going? He was about to work up the courage to ask when they turned onto a tiny road and drove up to an adobe house with a clay-tile roof on a small farm.

The Farmer shut off the engine and climbed out. He looked back at the boy. "Don't just sit there. Come on."

Parker took a deep breath and followed him to the front door.

The Farmer knocked and they waited.

"Maybe no one is home," suggested Parker.

The Farmer didn't seem to hear him.

They stood a minute more until an old man in denim opened the front door. Parker recognized the man's bushy gray mustache immediately.

The old man looked equal parts sad and surprised. "You came yourself."

"I'm afraid I have nothing to offer," said the Farmer. "But I thought we might stay with him for a while."

The old man looked like he was going to cry. His lip trembled before he opened the door wider. "I suppose that's only fair."

"Life isn't governed by fairness," said the Farmer. "Our actions aren't, either."

The old man forced a smile before pointing to a room in the back of the house. The Farmer tilted his head as he passed under the doorframe. Parker cautiously followed. The house was cozy. A few embers burned in a fireplace and a quilt was draped over a sofa. The Farmer reached the back room, knocked on the door, opened it, ducked, and entered. Parker let out an uneasy sigh as he followed the Farmer into a bedroom.

The bed took up most of the room. Sitting next to it was a familiar old woman wrapped in a shawl. She was knitting something blue. The woman peeked up at the Farmer and smiled. "It's you."

Parker's body stiffened when he saw Milo. The boy from the white truck lay asleep on top of the bed. Sweat covered Milo's brow despite the steady breeze from an open window. It was cold for summer.

Milo's skin was paler than Parker remembered. And the boy seemed smaller. Parker wondered if Milo had been sick when they first met.

The old woman stood. "Let me get you an extra chair and some blankets."

The Farmer nodded as the woman stepped out.

Parker glanced around uncomfortably. "What are we doing here?"

"What little we can." The Farmer gestured to the old woman's chair. "Sit."

Parker looked from the Farmer to Milo before warily taking a seat. The old woman returned with a stool and two quilts, handed them to the Farmer, and closed the door as she left.

The Farmer passed a quilt to Parker and sat on the opposite side of the bed. He wrapped himself in the blanket to stay warm and Parker did the same.

They watched Milo sleep.

Parker wasn't sure how long they sat there, but outside the room he heard the older couple start and finish dinner. Occasionally Parker stole glances at the Farmer. Sometimes the Farmer was watching Milo, but just as often the Farmer's eyes were closed.

The longer Parker looked at Milo the worse off he seemed. Finally he had to ask. "Shouldn't he be at a hospital or something?"

"There's nothing a doctor can do now. And nothing we can do, either. Just sit a little while longer."

"You mean—" Parker froze because he knew. And suddenly it became too difficult to keep his eyes open to look at the younger boy. So he closed them. A few minutes later he felt a hand on his shoulder.

He opened his eyes to find the Farmer standing over him. "We can go."

Parker's eyes darted to Milo. The younger boy slept.

~

The Farmer offered no words of comfort as they began the drive to the farm. Parker stared at him incredulously, waiting for an explanation. Nothing came, and Parker grew tired of waiting.

"Why did you take me there?"

The Farmer kept his eyes on the road. "Our actions have consequences."

"Consequences?"

"Some big and some small."

Parker shook his head. "I'm not following you."

"Take a moment and think, Parker. Then speak."

Parker frowned at the Farmer, sighed, and thought for a moment. "Are you telling me that it was Milo's dream to fly or something?"

The Farmer shook his head. "That boy can hardly

walk. The radishes only made you fly because you're healthy and their vigor had to be exerted somehow."

"I don't understand."

"Think."

Parker's head snapped back. "Wait. Are the radishes like medicine?"

"Not 'like,' Parker."

"This is the business you're in?"

"It's hardly a business. And I certainly don't do it for the money. We only charge what people can afford, which isn't enough to keep a farm running. Hence our need for benefactors and inexpensive labor."

Parker's mouth fell, and panic set in. "Well, we're growing more, right? Shouldn't we have new radishes in a couple of weeks?"

"The boy doesn't have that long."

Parker's world spun as the consequences of his actions caught up to him. "Can't we get one of the radishes you dropped off a few days ago? There were two truckloads."

The Farmer remained calm. "They're spoken for."

"All of them?" Parker's thoughts ran wild.

"Every one. Before we make a delivery the destination for each has been considered and debated."

"So you just decide who gets one and who doesn't?"

"I assure you it's not taken lightly."

Parker felt numb. "Why didn't you say something?"

"You were told not to eat the radishes, Parker. Eventually you'll likely be responsible for others in this world, but you'll need to start with yourself."

"Why are you talking to me like a fortune cookie?"

The Farmer watched the road.

Parker pressed on. "How can you be so calm about this?"

"I'm only calm on the outside."

Parker started to hyperventilate. The Farmer reached over and rolled down the passenger window. The chilly night air blew into Parker's face.

"Take a deep breath," said the Farmer.

Parker did, and then another.

"Good," said the Farmer. "Keep breathing."

"So—Are you—Are you saying Milo is going to die because of me?"

The Farmer shook his head. "You're not the one who made that boy sick."

Parker stared at the Farmer before turning to the vast sky above. Then his breathing slowed as he watched the headlights cut through the darkness, as the truck wound down dirt roads. And the next thing Parker knew, they were stopped in front of the barn.

"Are you okay?" asked the Farmer.

"That's not the word I would use."

The Farmer's hands rested on the steering wheel.

Parker took a breath to gather his thoughts and courage. "I know I haven't always been the best person, but I've been trying here, and I wish I could make things right. I want to be better."

The Farmer sighed. "Well, the good news is that how someone starts almost always matters less than how they finish. Finish strong, Parker. Goodnight."

Parker climbed out and closed the door, eyed the Farmer through the open window. "I'm sorry about what I did. I didn't know."

"I know you didn't. You're not the first person to let curiosity get the best of them. And you certainly won't be the last." The Farmer drove off to the garage.

———

Parker went inside and told the boys everything he'd learned and experienced. He wasn't sure how much Mingo was already aware of—perhaps some of it, maybe all of it—but that was the least of Parker's concerns.

The boys sat with heads hung. Seemingly as surprised and distraught as Parker.

"I had a feeling the radishes were for something like that," said Chet.

The others stared at him.

"How?" asked Walter.

Chet shrugged. "I have eyes and ears, man."

Parker smirked. Chet began pacing.

"I just can't wrap my head around the science of it," said Tyrone.

"You didn't understand how they could make you fly, either," said Carlos.

Tyrone turned to his friend. Thought for a moment. "You're right. And I'm sorry for doubting you in the past. I don't have the answers to everything. I only wish I knew what we were supposed to do now."

"I'm not sure there's anything to do," said Parker.

The boys struggled with their thoughts in silence until Chet called their attention to something out the back window. "Hey, check it out."

Everyone crowded Chet. Under the moonlight and stars a lone figure stood in the fourth pen.

"Is that Boss?" asked Carlos.

"He hasn't moved since I spotted him," said Chet.

"What do you think he's doing?" said Walter.

"Probably grappling with the weight of the world," said Parker.

The boys watched.

"How long you think he's planning on standing out there?" asked Chet.

"One way to find out." Parker made his way out of the barn, buttoning the top buttons of his flannel to stay warm as he crossed the field.

The Farmer stood firm.

Parker climbed the blue fence, then dug his hands into his pockets as he approached. He shuffled up next to the Farmer and gazed at the field with him.

Parker nearly jumped as something moved past his right shoulder. Chet had followed. And Mingo, Walter, Carlos, and Tyrone trailed him.

The six stood in a circle with the Farmer, and then they waited. Parker's gut told him it was best to stay quiet, be present, and listen. And that was when he heard the faintest sound.

Was that a raindrop?

He looked to the sky but saw nothing falling. He glanced at the Farmer as a tear trickled down the man's cheek and dropped to the soil.

Parker was so startled by the sight of the Farmer crying that he took a step back. He tried to think if he'd ever seen an adult cry. Certainly not one as big as the Farmer. Maybe his mother? He wasn't sure. It frustrated him that he could not remember.

He certainly couldn't recall seeing his father cry. Even after it became just the two of them at home. There were a couple of times when he caught his father leaving his bedroom with red eyes. He figured his mother being gone was just as hard on his dad as it was on him. Their house had been happier when she was there.

Watching the Farmer, Parker wished he'd told his father it was okay to cry in front of him. Talking about feelings had been easier when his mother was around. He never felt he was strong enough to do it without her, so he didn't. Instead, he did things like sneak ponies into movie theaters, irritate vice principals, and pour punch mix into swimming pools. As Parker watched the tears drip down the Farmer's cheeks, he realized he hadn't behaved that way because he was weak but because he was scared.

Before Parker knew it, he was crying, too. His mind raced through countless mistakes, missed opportunities, and poor decisions. And then Parker cried harder when he realized that Milo wouldn't be able to have any more regrets of his own.

When Parker looked around the circle, he discovered

that the others were also crying. Tears soaked the ground until there were no tears left to fall.

Then the Farmer turned and walked into his house, and one by one, the others returned to the barn.

Parker stood outside the longest.

He felt better, but he was far from fine.

And he wasn't convinced he would ever feel fine again.

He lay awake on his cot for the rest of the night.

24

THE NEXT MORNING Parker stared at the ceiling until a sliver of sunlight crept through the window. He felt drained and dazed, like his memories, thoughts, and feelings weren't his own.

He looked at the photo of his mother and worried he had let her down. That he had changed too much from the kid he used to be.

He needed fresh air.

He needed to leave the barn.

He needed to pull himself off his cot.

So he slipped on his clothes and tiptoed to the door with Outcast. Outside he found Molly waiting at the picnic table. Parker couldn't put his finger on how seeing her made him feel, but the closest word he could come up with was relieved.

"Heard you had an eventful evening," she said.

"I feel like dirt."

"Then cheer up. Even dirt has value. You should know that by now."

Parker's lip curled.

"Walk with me?" she continued.

Molly rose and began to stroll around the field, her notebook under an arm, Parker and the dog at her side.

"I'm supposed to be asleep a couple of blocks from the ocean right now," he said.

"Change of plans," said Molly.

"Change of plans."

"I bet this is the last place you thought you'd spend your summer."

"Hard to know what you don't know."

"Who would've thought you'd fit in so well?"

Parker laughed. "Come on..."

"I'm serious. You're like one of them now."

"One of them? Like you're not everyone's favorite?"

Molly rolled her eyes. "I'll never really be part of the group. I live in the farmhouse and sometimes have to tell everyone else what to do. They're all scared of me."

"No way. Well, maybe a little."

"Right…"

"But honestly, everyone likes it when you're around. You should hang out more." They walked in silence, eyes on the field, but before long, Parker found his drifting to her freckles. "I wish I knew more about you."

"What does that mean? Why are you looking at me like that?"

"Like what? I'm not. Why?" Parker eyed the ground. "I just mean I like hearing things about you."

"You know pretty much everything."

"No, I don't. You haven't exactly talked my ear off."

"This may surprise you, but not everyone lacks a filter between their mouths and their brains." Molly sighed. "I guess it's hard to share when I'm struggling to keep so much secret."

"Well, now I'm in on the secret."

"You've barely scratched the surface."

"Oh."

She took a deep breath. "He's not really my uncle. He took me in when no one else would."

"Yeah? Family friend?"

"Bighearted stranger. After my parents died, I ended up in a situation that wasn't so good, but luckily the right people noticed and brought me here about five years ago."

"Wow."

She said nothing.

He swallowed. "I lost my mom, too. Car accident. It was a few years ago. She was coming home from work." Parker felt a weight lift. Like he had been holding on to a secret all summer.

Molly didn't flinch. "I was wondering when you were going to say something."

"You knew?"

She shrugged.

Parker thought for a moment. "It's hard to talk about. Kind of the only thing that's hard for me to talk about? Everyone used to say I was the mini version of her. Straight A's. Super organized. Responsible. But ever since she—Now when I notice I'm being like my mom, I can't stop thinking about her. So, I kind of do the opposite? I know it's dumb. I just miss her so much."

He sighed. "I got her sense of humor, too. But I can't really let that go. It wouldn't be fair to the rest of the world."

Parker winked at Molly.

Molly shook her head. "Seems you didn't inherit her modesty."

"No. That's all me."

Molly smiled.

Parker frowned. "So Boss didn't know you as a baby?"

"What? No."

"Huh." Parker rubbed the back of his neck. "It's just that I saw that photo in the foyer and figured it was the two of you."

"In the house? My goodness, Parker, you broke *all* the rules."

"Yeah," he admitted guiltily.

"His son," she said.

"He has a kid? Does he live around here?"

Molly shook her head. "He's, uh, not..."

"Oh."

"Losing his son is what brought him to this life. Wanting as few people as possible to go through what he did. That pain drives him. I know not having my parents is what motivates me."

Parker and Molly walked until he couldn't hold on to the question that had been eating away at him any longer. "Where do the radishes come from?"

"Even I don't know that. But I figure it's less important where they're from and more important where they're going."

"And you decide where they're going? Is that what the newspapers are for?"

"Just one of the tools we use to find who needs a miracle." Molly flipped through her notebook. Newspaper articles were pasted to the pages, and handwritten notes covered the margins.

Parker was stunned. "It's almost full."

"I've gone through one hundred and fifty-three notebooks since I got here."

Parker processed the number. Shook his head in amazement. "So what do you do? Reach out to the families?"

"We work behind the scenes. He's been doing this long enough that he has folks all over the country who provide assistance and flood our phone lines with information about people who won't make it into a newspaper until it's too late. Plus, the locals have all heard the rumors and call us directly. We help when we can. I just wish we could help everyone."

"I can't imagine having to choose. How can you put the pressure of that kind of decision on yourself?"

"How can I not?"

Parker nodded, hung his head. "I feel horrible."

"Of course you do, you're bighearted, too."

"Why do you say that?"

"I can always spot the good ones right away." Molly tapped a fist against Parker's arm. "I have to get back to the phones."

She headed for the house.

"Hey, Molly?"

She turned.

"Thanks for telling me."

"What specifically?" she asked.

"All of it."

"You too. And now you can bear some of the load."
She forced a smile before heading off.

Parker's shoulders slumped. He walked in a haze
with the dog by his side as the sun became comfortable
in the sky. When they finished their trip around the
field, they rested against the fourth pen and gathered
strength to face the day.

Then Parker's eyes went wide.

⸻

The other boys were nearly finished getting ready when
the door to the barn flew open and Parker charged in.

"Did you guys reseed the fourth pen yesterday?"

"We're doing it today, man," said Chet.

"And we're laying two layers of soil," said Tyrone.

"Gonna be a long one, bud," said Mingo.

"You have to see this," announced Parker before
running back out.

By the time the others spilled from the barn Parker was already hopping the fence to the fourth pen.

"What are you doing?" called Carlos.

"He's become way too much of a morning person," said Walter.

"Over here," said Parker.

The others hustled after him until they were all squatting in the middle of the enclosure. Parker nodded toward the ground. "I thought they were weeds at first, but look at these."

Walter and the others stared at eleven two-inch leaves in three clusters sprouting from the field.

"Those look like—" said Tyrone.

"Those are radish leaves, man," said Chet.

"They sure are," said Mingo.

Parker smiled so widely it hurt.

25

THE FARMER GOT on his hands and knees for a closer look at the spot they had circled the night before. He brushed a finger against the sprouts. "These look like they'll be ready to pick in a day or two."

Parker and the others couldn't stop smiling. And for a split second, Parker thought he saw the corner of the Farmer's mouth curl up.

"How did we miss those?" asked Mingo. "They weren't there yesterday and now it looks like they've been growing a week longer than the radishes in the other three pens, but not as long as the crop we lost. I mean, how could that be?"

No one had a theory to share, but Parker felt confident that everyone knew.

Chet scratched his head. "What do we do about reseeding, Boss?"

The Farmer stood and admired the field. "You reseed." He pointed to the sprouts. "Just be careful around these."

And with that, the Farmer walked to the house and the boys went to work.

Each boy took a turn sitting next to the sprouts to make sure that none of the others accidentally trampled them. Every so often the radishes were spritzed with a spray bottle from the supply shed, and the first hints of any budding weeds were pulled. Meanwhile the others laid fresh seeds over the newly made rows and then sprinkled the topsoil that Mingo had bought from the store.

Eventually Molly joined the guys as her water system was carefully guided over the pen (Parker was placed on hose duty). After the field was watered, the boys sprinkled another light layer of topsoil and Mingo announced that they could call it a day. But Parker insisted on staying to look out for the radishes. The others felt it was only right to have a rotating guard. Then Molly suggested they all watch out for them together—as a group, which made Parker smile.

So that night Parker, Molly, and the boys carried cots to the field and arranged them a safe distance from the sprouts. Under the stars they talked, and laughed, and for the first time felt truly together.

"Hey, Molly?" said Chet.

"Yes?"

"This is a good summer. Much better than sitting on my grandmother's couch."

"Thanks, Chet."

"It's a pretty nice couch, too."

"We assumed," said Parker.

"Is that why Boss invited me here?" asked Chet. "To get me off the couch?"

"Kind of," said Molly. "He's the most empathetic person I've ever met. He gave you a new path. Just like he gave me. That's what he does. Not just with the radishes, but with all of this for us. And whoever else he can give a second chance, or recalibration."

"What about Tyrone and me?" said Carlos.

Molly smiled at Carlos and Tyrone. "Well, you guys would've been fine. But I think he figures we always need at least a couple smart and responsible people to make this place run smoothly."

"Wise of the man," said Tyrone.

Walter stared at Molly. Seemingly wrestling with whether he wanted to say something. He took a deep breath. "I think I know the answer, but what about me?"

"I figure you're just here to make some friends," said Molly.

Walter pursed his lips.

"Can't imagine you need help in that department," said Parker. "You're so welcoming and accommodating."

Walter chuckled, then laid his head on his pillow. "I guess friends are the one thing that money can't buy."

Parker looked at Walter, nodded toward the group. "Now you don't need to worry about it."

As the others drifted to sleep, Walter propped himself back up on his cot and whispered, "Hey, Big City, my aunt was right about you."

—

The Farmer shook Parker awake in the field the next morning. The sun had risen and the others were eating breakfast.

"It's time," said the Farmer. "They grew faster than I thought possible."

Parker stared up at the Farmer and gathered his bearings. The Farmer stuck out a hand and helped him off the cot. Parker wiped the sleep from his eyes.

The two walked to the radishes and kneeled. The Farmer pulled a hand fork from his back pocket and held it out for Parker.

Parker shook his head. "You should do it."

"Finish strong, Parker," said the Farmer.

Parker took the hand fork and paused a second to examine the leaves growing from the ground. He stuck the fork into the soil and gently removed three radishes. Brushed away the dirt.

The radishes were twice the size of the ones they'd harvested a few days earlier. Parker had never seen anything so beautiful. He placed the hand fork back into the earth and cradled the plants.

"Let's go," said the Farmer.

Parker took a deep breath, then stood and followed the Farmer out of the pen and toward the house. He exchanged nods with Carlos, Tyrone, Walter, and Mingo as he passed. Chet waved as he scratched Outcast behind the ears.

When they reached the garage, Parker found Molly sitting in the red pickup. Parker opened the passenger door and held out the radishes for her.

"Do I give these to you?" he asked.

Molly shook her head. "Get in."

Parker nodded and squeezed in next to her as the Farmer got behind the wheel.

The truck eased out of the garage and down the dirt road.

Parker didn't take his eyes off the radishes in his lap the entire drive. As he gently rolled them between his fingers, he was surprised by how sturdy his hands were. His soft skin had become strong.

The instant the truck pulled up to the adobe house, the old man anxiously stepped out onto the porch. The Farmer held a massive palm across the cab and Parker placed the three radishes in it. Then the Farmer got out and walked to the house. Parker strained to hear what the Farmer said to the old man, but he only heard the

231

wind. Then the radishes were handed over and the old man hugged the Farmer. The men exchanged a few more words before the old man disappeared into the house, closing the door behind him.

Parker watched as the Farmer stood on the porch for a moment before making his way back behind the wheel. The truck turned toward the farm.

Parker looked from Molly to the Farmer for some kind of explanation. "Will he be okay?"

"We all will." The Farmer leaned over and put a hand on Parker's shoulder. "Strong finish."

26

PARKER STOOD IN front of his dresser tossing clothes into a backpack. His tan was long gone, but his vintage Hawaiian shirt with its pink floral pattern made up for his lack of color. He lifted the photograph of his mother off the wall and carefully slipped it in his bag for a new summer adventure.

Mr. Kelbrook knocked before poking his head into the bedroom. His neck jerked when he saw his son. "Oh. You're up. Was just coming to say goodbye."

Parker threw a couple of swimsuits into his bag. "I thought I could catch a ride with you. Maybe help wash and wax the cars?"

"Really? You don't want to spend your last morning in town with your friends?"

Parker shrugged. "Nah. Figure it's probably easier for Kevin and Mrs. Levy to pick me up at Ms. Birdseye's anyway."

"Yeah?" Mr. Kelbrook nodded, impressed. "Great."

"And maybe we could swing by and see Mom on the way?"

Mr. Kelbrook smiled. "Of course."

Parker stepped to his desk and picked up a loose bouquet of flowers. Soil fell from the roots. "I got these for her."

"Wow. Where did those come from?"

"Flower bed across the street. The neighbors with the dog that barks all night?"

"Huh. You really shouldn't do that."

"It's what Mom would have wanted."

Mr. Kelbrook shook his head, stepped into the room, and adjusted his jumpsuit's collar in Parker's mirror. "You about ready?"

Parker zipped his backpack. "Ready. All right if I drive?"

"Absolutely not."

⌒

Ms. Birdseye eyed her newspaper as she grabbed a crescent roll from one of the platters spread across her dining room table. "Well, another year of school completed. Perhaps you've grown a year wiser?"

Parker shoved bacon into his mouth as he reached for a jelly donut. "I'm at least taller."

"I suppose that's better than nothing."

"Give me some credit, Ms. Birdseye. Growth spurts are exhausting and I haven't had a nap this morning."

Ms. Birdseye smiled and shook her head. "I suppose you can sleep on your journey."

"Can and will."

Ms. Birdseye set her newspaper on the table. "Parker, I have to say, you've surprised me."

"With my amazing charm?"

"Constantly. But I was referring to your summer plans."

Parker shrugged. "I need to reset and recharge."

"Fair enough. I guess you've earned it. I'll never be able to repay you for making my nephew tolerable. You know I had a telephone call with him this week and he told me an honest-to-goodness joke?"

"The rusty shovel made you laugh?"

"I didn't say it was a good joke, but it was nice to be reminded that not all rust is permanent."

A smirk crept across Parker's face. "My mom always found the good in people."

Ms. Birdseye smiled. "That she did. The rest of the staff always had such pep and spark because of her. It was a cheerier home. She wasn't just my assistant; she was my best friend."

"Mine too."

She nodded. "I'll miss you, young man."

"And I you, Ms. Birdseye. But summer will be over before you know it. Don't do anything I wouldn't do."

"I can't imagine what that could even be."

~

The back seat of the station wagon was littered with fast-food wrappers and empty bags of potato chips. Parker slept with his face against a window. His Hawaiian shirt was covered in cookie crumbs and a small stain from an incident with a cherry cola the night before.

Kevin sat across from him applying sunscreen. His red shorts were arguably a size too small, but he didn't look too bad in his black T-shirt and sunglasses. When he finished rubbing the lotion into his arms he leaned over and shook Parker awake. "Hey. We're almost there. Want to put on some sunblock?"

Parker took in his surroundings, then took the bottle from Kevin with an appreciative nod.

"Morning, sleepyhead," called Kevin's mother from behind the wheel.

"Morning," said Parker as he spread the sunscreen.

"I can't believe we finally get to spend the summer together," said Kevin.

Parker grinned as the station wagon came to a stop.

Kevin looked out his window. "Well, definitely bigger than last year's beach house."

"I'm proud of you boys," said Kevin's mother.

"Thanks for the ride, Mrs. Levy," said Parker as he grabbed his backpack, gave Kevin a punch on the arm, and climbed out of the car in front of the farmhouse.

It was warmer than he remembered. Not hot, pleasant. And everything seemed brighter. The house, barn, and new water tower had fresh coats of green paint. The fence a fresh coat of blue. And the sprouts in the pens appeared more vibrant than before. It all felt alive.

Off in the field Parker spotted Chet and Walter with a couple of boys he didn't know. Outcast happily dug a hole next to them. Chet looked bigger and more confident as he gave instructions to the new kids. Walter's hair had grown out, and he gave a friendly wave when he saw Parker. As Parker waved back he got a better look at one of the new kids: Milo. He seemed taller, too.

Parker beamed, then glanced up at the farmhouse to see the Farmer peering down from his office. Parker nodded and the man nodded back. Then the Farmer smiled before turning away.

"Traveling light?"

Parker looked over to see Molly making her way toward the house. Her hair was in a ponytail and her freckles were just as he remembered. He glanced down at the backpack dangling from his hand, shrugged. "I figured I could borrow hand-me-downs again."

"That's presumptuous."

"Thank you."

"That wasn't a compliment."

"Anything can be a compliment if you take it the right way."

"You're a ridiculous person."

"Occasionally I can be an acquired taste." Parker gestured with his head to his friend saying goodbye to his mother at the station wagon. "That's Kevin."

"Obviously."

"It's good to see you," said Parker.

"I know it is," she said as she approached the back door. Then she glanced over her shoulder. "I'm glad you're back."

"Me too."

The station wagon honked as Kevin's mom drove away.

"You have sunscreen all over your nose," said Molly as she pulled open the door.

Parker shook his head as she went inside, then rubbed in the lotion on his face. Kevin pulled his luggage up next to Parker and stared as the door closed behind Molly.

"I think I get why you like this place," said Kevin.

"You don't," said Parker. "But you will."

"Should we unpack and get settled?"

"We should probably just drop our stuff off and get started. It's Monday."

"What happens on Monday?"

"On Mondays we pull weeds."

Kevin frowned. "Seriously?"

"Why would I joke about pulling weeds?"

"I can't believe you didn't want to go to the beach."

Parker patted his friend on the shoulder and stared at the field. "This is better than wasting a summer at the ocean."

Kevin scratched the back of his head. "How?"

"You'll see."

ACKNOWLEDGMENTS

This book was edited by Alexandra Hightower. The best ideas came from her. Massive thanks to Megan Tingley, Alvina Ling, and everyone at Little, Brown Books for Young Readers. Special thanks to Mercè López, Sam Kalda, Marisa Finkelstein, Marisa Russell, Shivani Annirood, Jenny Kimura, Brittany Groves, Emilie Polster, Shanese Mullins, Mara Brashem, and Christie Michel.

I am represented by the wonderful Janine Kamouh. Janine's and James Munro's fingerprints were all over the outlining and development of this book. Thanks to them and the amazing team at WME, especially Alicia Everett, Sabrina Taitz, Danny Greenberg, Olivia Burgher, Oma Naraine, Ty Anania, and Laura Bonner.

Endless thanks to my family. For everything.

Tons of gratitude to Andy Kimble, Clara Hoffmann, Jim Whitaker, Stephanie Varela Rheingold, and Steve Nuchols for early reads and helpful notes. To Jordan Hoffmann, Adam Levy, David Lowery,

Toby Halbrooks, Ava DuVernay, Jonathan Auxier, and Brad Montague—thank you for your friendships and inspiration.

Huge thanks to all the terrific teachers and librarians that I've encountered along the way. And that you've encountered along your way.

Most importantly, thank you to my wife, Erin Malone. She's my favorite person and storyteller.

Turn the page for a sneak preview of

The Midnight Brigade

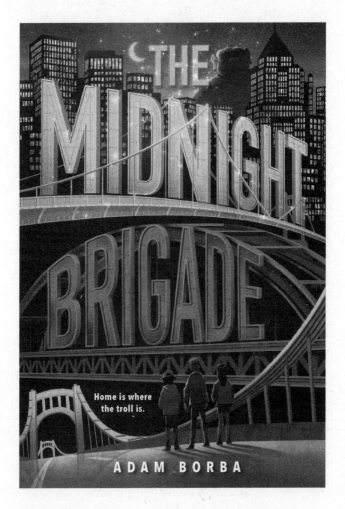

Available in paperback September 2022

PROLOGUE

C arl's parents were fighting again the first night it happened. Mr. and Mrs. Chesterfield fought about everything. Misunderstandings. Facts. Opinions. Neglected chores. If it was possible to squabble about something, Carl's parents did. They hadn't always been this way. But lately, Carl's father was less than happy at work, and he often brought that unhappiness home.

When his parents shouted and stomped around their bedroom, the pale-blue wall separating their room from his shook and the ancient ceiling fan above him rattled. As Carl gripped his sheets, he worried the vibrations would cause the rickety old thing to crash down on him. Why would anyone put a fan above a bed, he wondered. It seemed specifically intended to cause insomnia and nightmares.

Whenever the fighting got bad, Carl would sit on his windowsill and count bridges. There was something soothing about a sturdy bridge. He could see quite a few from his second-story perch. Thirty-three, to be exact. He took comfort in that number (though not enough comfort to stop worrying about his parents).

Then he saw it. At first he thought his parents' yelling and stomping were to blame, but he quickly decided that was impossible. A bridge wobbled. Teetered a foot to the left, then back again. Like a squirrel poking its head around a tree. Only for a moment. But bridges shouldn't move at all, at least not a bridge made from hundreds of tons of Pittsburgh steel. What could cause such a thing? He stared at the bridge until his mother yelled, "Something has to change!" Then his parents went quiet. Carl dared the bridge to budge again. Had his eyes played a trick on him? Must have, he thought as he climbed into bed. Then, as he drifted to sleep, he could've sworn he heard something deep in the city growl in pain.

———◆———

Carl's father's side of the family had lived in Pittsburgh for five generations. Mr. Chesterfield was an engineer by trade and a bridge builder in practice. Carl thought Pittsburgh was as good a place as any for a bridge builder to live. The city had over four hundred bridges, and dozens of those had been built by Carl's father and his father before him, and Carl's great-grandfather before that. Bridge building was a noble profession, allowing Pittsburghers to travel from one end of something to the other end of something else. Without a bridge, they would be forced to go around.

Unfortunately, after a city has constructed over four hundred bridges, few places remain for new bridges to be built. So, rather than building new bridges, Carl's dad mostly repaired old ones. But bridge *repairing* wasn't what he had signed up for. Instead of designing something new, he now restored and replicated someone else's work. He missed creating. Missed making his own decisions.

Recently, the bridges in Pittsburgh needed to be repaired at a curiously high rate. Not astronomically higher than bridges elsewhere, but enough that it was noticeable to the people who kept track of that sort of thing. It troubled Carl. It also kept Mr. Chesterfield busy at work, only his heart wasn't in it. Carl's father needed to find a new noble profession. But what do Pittsburghers need as much as traveling from one end of something to the other end of something else? He pondered this aloud with his son on a Sunday stroll. It was cold for late February, but their puffy coats and Mr. Chesterfield's ability to make Carl laugh helped. Like when he rubbed his coat's sleeves against his sides to make record-scratching sounds or pretended he could only move in slow motion. As they talked, they pulled out and unwrapped two peanut butter and tomato sandwiches. And after they'd taken bites, made faces, then tossed their less-than-tasty sandwiches into the trash, something caught Mr. Chesterfield's eye.

In the trash can beneath the hardly eaten sandwiches was a newspaper with two classified ads that had been overlooked by all other Pittsburghers—two seemingly unrelated ads that would set the Chesterfield family on a life-altering path.

The first ad was for a quarter acre of land under one of Pittsburgh's oldest bridges—one that Carl's great-grandfather had helped build. The second ad was for a food truck with a busted engine and blown tires—one that had a "decently working kitchen with limited assembly required" (rust included—no extra charge). Mr. Chesterfield explained that the ads must have been placed specifically for him. And he was never wrong (except for the times when he was).

Carl did his best to unpack those thoughts as they crossed the street to a diner. He was reasonably certain two separate ads wouldn't target his father. But not wanting to rock the boat, Carl simply gave a supportive nod and listened to his dad ramble while an uneasy feeling grew inside him.

As the diner's waiter delivered plates of burgers and fries, Carl's father announced that he would buy the food truck and open it on that quarter acre of land. "What's more noble than feeding the masses?" he asked as he smacked ketchup out of a bottle and onto his plate. "It's the perfect job for me," he proclaimed.

Carl said nothing but knew his father was mistaken. Mr. Chesterfield had made the peanut butter and tomato sandwiches.

While Mr. Chesterfield boasted about how successful his soon-to-be-launched truck would be, Carl worried about the bridges his father would no longer repair. Why did they need to be repaired so often? And had that bridge outside his window actually moved?

His father sighed and explained that the damage wasn't typical wear and tear caused by Pittsburghers using the bridges to travel from one end of something to the other end of something else. The repairs needed to be done to damage that seemed intentional. And there was no way Carl had seen a bridge move—"Our bridges have been built expertly, by *Chesterfields*."

"Won't you, uh, miss working on them?" asked Carl.

"They'll be fine," said Mr. Chesterfield, scooping up his hamburger. Carl watched as his father took a chomp and continued to describe the damage, huffing with disdain. "It *is* annoying, though. Chunks of steel ripped in the night, and rows and rows of deep scratches..."

It all seemed like the opposite of fine to Carl, whose stomach dropped as he watched his father chew.

"Like, um, something's taking bites out of them?" asked Carl.

"Bites? I guess that's one way to put it. It's all disrespectful, really."

"But who?" Carl wondered. Mr. Chesterfield had no answer. And to Carl's disappointment, his father didn't seem interested in finding out either. But Carl was.

That's when Carl began to suspect that Pittsburgh was secretly overrun by monsters.

CHAPTER ONE

C arl hadn't slept since the night he saw the bridge move. Wherever he went, he had the feeling he'd just missed a monster out of the corner of his eye. But his lack of sleep gave him plenty of time to search for answers. He looked up the word *monster* in the dictionary (it wasn't that useful). He checked under his bed and in his closet. And he spent countless hours gazing out his window at the city.

Meanwhile, his father had set out to obtain a loan to start his new business. Mr. Chesterfield didn't think borrowing money would be an issue. As he told Carl, he had eaten three meals a day for nearly forty years, and if that didn't qualify him to launch his own food enterprise, what would? The twenty-one banks he visited saw things differently.

"You need relevant experience," said one bank.

"You don't even know how to cook," said another.

"You're just so incredibly average," sighed the twenty-first.

And that was all the motivation Mr. Chesterfield needed. He was *average*. Incredibly so! He excitedly explained to his son that if he liked something, "then by golly so will the average customer. If the banks won't give me a loan, I'll just find the money another way." Mr. Chesterfield was certain he had the instincts of the everyman, and that his food truck was bound to be a smashing success.

———————◆———————

Carl's mother disagreed. And she was the rational parent, so it was hard for Carl not to silently take her side during dinner in the family's old town house.

"You've lost your mind," said Mrs. Chesterfield.

"My plan is foolproof," said Mr. Chesterfield.

"Any plan you had would *have* to be foolproof," mumbled Mrs. Chesterfield. "How did you even convince a bank to give you a loan?"

"I took out a second mortgage instead," said Mr. Chesterfield.

Carl wasn't sure what that meant, but by the way his mother's face fell he knew that it wasn't good, so he sank into his chair.

"Are you joking?" asked Mrs. Chesterfield.

"There's no need to overreact," replied Mr. Chesterfield. "What's the big deal?"

Carl attempted to sink lower as he watched his mother's fingernails dig into the dining room table. "The big deal is that I've become accustomed to sleeping with a roof over our heads, and now you're risking our home so you can borrow money to sell food when you can barely prepare your own cereal."

Carl was used to his parents fighting, but that didn't mean he liked it. So as the argument continued, he slid all the way out of the chair and headed upstairs. As he closed the door to his room, he heard his mother shout at his father, "I can't believe you kept this a secret from me until now!"

Carl's parents were wonderful at keeping secrets. As far as he could tell, they knew little about each other beyond the obvious:

Mr. Chesterfield had wiry muscles and sun-kissed skin from decades of building things outside with his hands, and a mustache that made up for the hair he was losing on his head.

Mrs. Chesterfield wore her hair up in a perfect bun and possessed the confident chin and posture of a former ballerina.

Financially, they were in over their heads.

And they loved their son very much.

———◆———

Like most kids, Carl had a limited understanding of real estate law. Listening to his parents yell through the walls, he determined that since they had "closed escrow," they now officially owned that underdeveloped patch of land downtown. His father said it was an ideal location for his new business. His mother said his father was an idiot.

The yelling made sleep more difficult than ever. Because Carl didn't have any art or photographs on his walls to stare at, he spent the evening counting the rotations of his rickety ceiling fan in an attempt to keep his mind off the fighting.

Two hours after the argument began, it came to a sudden stop and Carl heard water running, which he knew meant his mother had taken a break to brush her teeth. Mrs. Chesterfield was a dental hygienist at the city's most respected practice for cleanings and oral surgery. She told Carl that teeth had been her passion since she was a little girl. She flossed twice a day and never had to lie about it. But lately Carl noticed that his mother had been losing her enthusiasm for teeth besides her own. He suspected that years of hearing how much patients dreaded coming for appointments had worn her down, and that she couldn't understand why others didn't love brushing as much as she did. Still, his mother continued working because there were bills to pay. He knew she wanted the best for him. Though neither of them seemed to know what that was. Meanwhile his father had secretly quit working as soon as the check from their second mortgage arrived. He presumed *he* knew best. Carl doubted that was the case.

Carl's father took a detour on the drive to school the next morning because the bridge they typically used to cross the Monongahela River was closed for repairs. "Haven't seen a shutdown of that one in my life," mumbled Mr. Chesterfield as he drummed on the steering wheel. Carl swore he saw teeth marks on the bridge as they drove past. He worried that the clues supporting a monster infestation were piling up.

A few blocks later, Mr. Chesterfield pulled in front of Carl's school. Carl thanked his father for the ride, took a deep breath, and climbed out to face the day.

Carl Chesterfield was the shortest boy in his class. He had pencil-thin arms and holes in all his jeans. His straight, dark hair was cut by his mother. He didn't have friends. His mom's awful haircuts didn't help. His shyness didn't either. Carl was a mediocre student and generally overlooked by his classmates, but he had one special skill—Carl was an excellent observer. He was the first to notice when someone got new clothes. To recognize who was out sick. To pick up on who was having a great day, or who was feeling sad. He watched. He listened. He processed. He empathized. He formed conclusions. And above all, he worried. About his parents. About strangers. About himself. But he never shared his insights or concerns with anyone. He wanted to, but what if the person he told didn't care? What then?

As an observer, he was the first (and perhaps only) student

to notice the turquoise flyer on the bulletin board on the way to lunch:

SOMETHING IS RAVAGING
OUR BRIDGES, PEOPLE.
STAY ALERT.

CORDIALLY,
THE MB

Carl couldn't believe it. Was someone playing a joke on him? He hadn't told his theory to anyone, so how could they? Perhaps somebody actually shared his fear. He scratched his head as he wondered who The MB was. He couldn't recall having a class with anyone who had those initials. He wished he knew who had posted the flyer. Maybe that person could be a friend.

As usual, Carl was among the first students in the cafeteria, a room that always smelled of sloppy joes and all-purpose cleaner. It had been months since sloppy joes were even on the menu. Carl was never slowed by conversation on his way to lunch. Sometimes kids would snicker at his hair in the hall, but that was typically the extent of his social interaction. Mostly Carl felt invisible, which made him feel more safe than sad. Though today was different. Today, when he saw Teddy—the skinny, pale kid with all the freckles and floppy red hair, who always wore the same orange windbreaker—Teddy brought a finger to his lips and shushed him. Teddy was weird.

Carl always sat at the cafeteria's center table with open seats on either side of him, and open they would remain. Students would often eat across from Carl, but that wasn't the same as sitting with him. They'd talk to friends on their left or on their right—just never on the other side of the table, to Carl. The lunchroom, however, was a great place for Carl to observe. He was so caught up in observation that he didn't register the girl with the backward baseball cap slipping into a seat next to him. He'd seen the girl before but never noticed her, which is a distinction both small and enormous.

"Hey, Quiet Kid," she whispered. "Hold this for me."

Carl looked down to see a green metallic marker in a fist under the table. Without hesitating, he took the marker and slipped it into a pocket in his jeans. Then he looked up to see the smirk on her face. He locked eyes with the girl long enough to notice that hers were hazel.

"Thanks, Quiet Kid."

And with that she slipped away, leaving Carl to wonder.

There was a commotion outside the cafeteria after lunch. An ocean of students packed the hall. Carl pushed his way through the crowd, anxious to observe.

Principal Wilkinson was a stout man in his late fifties with a red face. This afternoon his face was redder than usual. Clearly he took issue with *Principal Wilkinson is a creep* scrawled across the not-quite-yellow eighth-grade lockers in metallic green. And perhaps he took more issue with the doodle of him below the insult. Though it was skillfully drawn, the doodle's artist had been less than flattering with Wilkinson's face.

"It wasn't me," said the girl with the backward baseball cap.

"Then who?" Principal Wilkinson asked. His pointer finger inches from her face, beads of sweat forming on his brow.

She pulled her pants pockets inside out. "Someone else who thinks you're a creep, I guess?"

The crowd gasped as Principal Wilkinson's face went from red to scarlet. He shook his head, patted a hand on the back of his neck.

"Back to class. Everyone."

The girl in the baseball cap and the rest of the crowd turned on their heels and made their ways from the lockers. Carl stood a moment longer. He'd never seen a man's head explode and feared this might be his only opportunity. You could hear a pin drop in the hallway. So of course Principal Wilkinson heard that green metallic marker hit the linoleum after it fell through a hole in the pocket of Carl's jeans.

Carl's invisibility had worn off.

On the surface, Principal Wilkinson's office was underwhelming. As a shy boy who kept to himself, Carl had never had the opportunity to be called to a principal's office. He'd always imagined it as more of a police interrogation room. Two-way mirror. A steel table with handcuffs in the middle. A no-nonsense older detective in the corner who doesn't "have time for *it* anymore." But this was just a cramped room with the same wooden desk his teachers had—only this desk had a very angry principal on the opposite side of it, and that very angry principal made the room much scarier than it would have been otherwise.

"I've never been so disrespected in my life," said the principal. "And you damaged school property. What do you have to say for yourself?"

Carl wondered if the principal could hear his heart pounding. He gulped and stared at Wilkinson for some time before he realized the man wouldn't speak again until he replied. It had been a while since Carl had said *anything* for himself to anyone other than his parents. He was somewhat out of his depth. And the room seemed to be spinning, which was unhelpful.

"I'm, um, sorry?"

"So, you admit it?"

"I do."

The words surprised Carl more than they did the principal. It was at that moment that Carl realized he had a crush on the girl with the backward baseball cap. And it was a moment later that Principal Wilkinson suspended Carl from school for the next two weeks.

Erin Borba

ADAM BORBA

is also the author of *The Midnight Brigade*. When he's not writing, he helps develop and produce movies for Walt Disney Studios. He is a graduate of Palm Springs High School, the University of Southern California, and the William Morris Agency mailroom. Adam lives in California with his family. *Outside Nowhere* is his second novel.